S0-AIJ-610

"He assumed we were lovers..."

Shrugging, she added carelessly, "My brother was taunting me, and I could see nothing was going to change his mind."

She'd known Nick would be angry, but she hadn't known how much his anger would hurt.

"Times are changing, Lucilla," he told her cruelly, "and I don't find it the least bit flattering to be linked with a woman who's reputed to have been to bed with every man who's ever offered her a job."

With less than a hundred savage words he'd ripped apart her defences and left her torn. She felt lonelier than she'd ever felt in her life. And he wasn't finished.

"The next time you tell anyone you and I are lovers, you'd better be able to back that claim..."

FRANCES RODING is a new name in the Harlequin romance series. However, we feel sure that the writing style of this British-based author will soon make her popular with romance readers everywhere.

Books by Frances Roding

HARLEQUIN PRESENTS
1052—OPEN TO INFLUENCE
2901—SOME SORT OF SPELL
1163—MAN OF STONE

Don't miss any of our special offers. Write to us at the following address for information on our newest releases.

Harlequin Reader Service
901 Fuhrmann Blvd., P.O. Box 1397, Buffalo, NY 14240
Canadian address: P.O. Box 603,
Fort Erie, Ont. L2A 5X3

FRANCES RODING

a different dream

Harlequin Books

TORONTO • NEW YORK • LONDON
AMSTERDAM • PARIS • SYDNEY • HAMBURG
STOCKHOLM • ATHENS • TOKYO • MILAN

Harlequin Presents first edition July 1989
ISBN 0-373-11190-8

Original hardcover edition published in 1988
by Mills & Boon Limited

Copyright © 1988 by Frances Roding. All rights reserved.
Except for use in any review, the reproduction or utilization
of this work in whole or in part in any form by any electronic,
mechanical or other means, now known or hereafter invented,
including xerography, photocopying and recording,
or in any information storage or retrieval system, is forbidden without
the permission of the publisher, Harlequin Enterprises Limited,
225 Duncan Mill Road, Don Mills, Ontario, Canada M3B 3K9.

All the characters in this book have no existence outside the
imagination of the author and have no relation whatsoever to
anyone bearing the same name or names. They are not even
distantly inspired by any individual known or unknown to the
author, and all incidents are pure invention.

® are Trademarks registered in the United States Patent and
Trademark Office and in other countries.

Printed in U.S.A.

CHAPTER ONE

THE WALLS of the hotel's ballroom had mirrored panels set in gilded rococo frames, in a style vaguely reminiscent of the heyday of the palace of Versailles; several other women had paused discreetly on the threshold of the room, surreptitiously checking their reflections, but Lucilla was the only one to stop and openly study her appearance.

It was perfect, of course. She had already known that; from the long, naturally blonde hair that framed her face, through the skilfully applied make-up that drew attention to her delicate bone-structure and striking colour, down the long svelte lines of her enviably slender five-foot-eight height, her body tonight dramatically sheathed in a clinging wrap dress of pure white silk that faithfully revealed every feminine curve, she was perfection personified. An ideal come to life.

But then, of course, she had known that without looking.

From the day she had realised that what she wanted most from life was to follow in the footsteps of her famous mother and become an actress, she had known how very important presentation and packaging was.

Tonight she looked every inch the successful soap opera star, which was exactly the image she had wanted to project. All those other hopefuls who had come here tonight, desperate for a chance to prove to Johns Cassavar how right they were for the role of leading female character in his new and much publicised soap opera, were going to to be disappointed.

The part was hers . . . It had to be . . . Her eyes, a dark, intense blue, closer to the brilliant density of sapphires than to the soft lighter shades normally common to English colouring, flashed. She caught sight of herself in the mirror again as she swayed elegantly into the room and frowned. Her tension was showing . . . She couldn't afford to appear doubtful. Success bred success, and all her life she had promised herself that the illustrious crown once worn by her mother must automatically descend to herself.

Who was there, after all, to challenge her right to it?

Beatrice, her elder half-sister, plain and dull and now deliriously happily married to Elliott, her half-brother? Mirry—the next to the youngest of the Bellaire clan.

She frowned again as she recalled her last meeting with Mirry. It had been last Christmas . . . A duty visit to Elliott and Beatrice's Cotswold home. Mirry, already established in her chosen career as a stage-costume designer had taunted her with the fact that, despite everything—her undeniable looks, her parentage, her burning desire to suceed—she was still not getting roles anywhere near as good as those that were already falling to her younger twin siblings.

She tossed her head and determinedly dismissed her family from her mind. Ben and Seb had set their sights on the RSC and what was to Lucilla's mind the dull drudgery of stage work.

That was not for her. She wanted fame, glamour . . . adulation. She wanted what she had been born for, and this role as Tabitha in John Cassavar's new soap would give them all to her . . .

And she would get it . . . She *had* to get it.

As she walked into the ballroom, set out this evening with tables and chairs around the outside of the polished floor to accommodate the guests at this very private party, she refused to acknowledge what her agent had already told her when she had demanded that he get her an invitation to the party, and that was that Tabitha St Alban at the start of the series was only sixteen years old.

And she was twenty-eight . . . Older, by at least half a dozen years, than the majority of the other women present here tonight. Her full mouth tightened in resentment and dislike.

She wanted this part . . . She needed it.

She swallowed a little, tension gripping her again. Since when had she ever needed anything or anyone? And why was it that with all her advantages —her looks, her family background, her ambition— she was still playing the same kind of bit parts she had started out on when she left drama school?

In those ten years her fellow students had in the main fallen by the wayside, leaving the profession to earn their livelihoods elsewhere. There were a few exceptions—contemporaries who had made it to the top.

And she should have been there with them . . . Leading them.

She remembered how scornful she had been of their dreams at drama school. She had been so convinced that for her it would be easy . . . After all, she was the daughter of Cressida Bellaire, the adored stepdaughter of her husband Charles—the husband from whom Cressida had been divorced before she married Lucilla's natural father, and then remarried later after Lucilla's father's death.

Lucilla dwelt for a moment on the tangled inter-family relationships which had led to her half-sister Beatrice marrying her stepbrother Elliot, and then dismissed them from her mind. That was old history, something that had happened over two years ago. This was now . . .

She searched the room, her eyes narrowing like a cat's when she found the person she was looking for.

John Cassavar was quite unmistakable. Six foot four and fairly heavily built, he was standing next to a table surrounded by half a dozen hovering acolytes. Her mouth curled disdainfully as she watched.

She could almost hear the fatuous words falling from their lips. John Cassavar at forty-six was already a wealthy man, an entrepreneur turned film-company owner. He had a Midas touch where his work was concerned, and the news that his company was to launch a new soap opera, the first major new soap for three years, had brought the theatrical world flocking to the Grosvenor to meet him.

The new soap was to have a historical background and would be set in Tudor England, following the fortunes of a wealthy landowning family, ambitious for honours and more wealth, vulnerable through their greed to the malice of England's King. The heroine, Tabitha St Alban, was to be sixteen years old in the first episode, and she would age to over eighty as it progressed. A demanding role, and one which John Cassavar had let it be known he wanted filled by an actress with an English accent.

Not for him the time-honoured Hollywood tradition of casting American actresses, complete with American accent, into period roles.

The part was perfect for her. Like every other ambitious actress in London, Lucilla had managed to get hold of a script. She could feel her skin start to burn with a mixture of tension and need.

Max had refused to get her an audition. He had told her gruffly that he didn't think she was right for the part, and when she had pressed him for a reason he had told her bluntly. 'You're too old, Lucilla. Too . . . worldly.'

She had been furious with him and had stormed out of his office vowing to find herself another agent, but he had been her mother's agent and he had an enviable reputation. Luckily his secretary hadn't been there when he had refused to get her an audition, and poor Matty, who Lucilla suspected had once been half in love with her charismatic stepfather, had quite happily agreed to send her one of the precious invitations to tonight's 'do' when she had rung up and pretended that Max had forgotten to give it to her.

Max would be furious with her, of course, but he wasn't going to be here tonight. He was in America himself. She wondered maliciously which little starlet her ticket had been intended for, and then dismissed the girl from her mind as her excellent antennae informed her that she was being watched.

Not by John Cassavar though, she noted, disappointed, as she swept his table with a discreet glance.

Who, then?

A bold search of the room soon told her. He was leaning against one of the marble pillars, dark and indolent, looking as though he would rather be anywhere but here. If she had one flaw, Lucilla acknowledged, it was that she was slightly short-sighted, and so it was impossible for her to tell exactly what colour his eyes were under the straight black brows. He moved his head, returning her open appraisal. He had a strong profile and a very stubborn jawline. He wasn't an actor, Lucilla knew that. He was too detached, too much the observer rather than the participator, and yet he would have made an excellent Sir Walter, the main male lead in the series.

He was still looking at her and, despite her shortsightedness, Lucilla was instinctively aware that something about her amused him.

She wasn't used to that kind of male reaction. Men had always desired her, for her looks and for the wealth she had been left by her natural father; but marriage, children . . . they weren't what she wanted from life. She wanted—craved success. It was an insatiable appetite inside her; a need that had never been appeased. Ever since she could remember she had had this desperate desire to come first, to be the most important . . . and she had bitterly resented her half-brothers and sisters, but one day they would have to acknowledge that she was better than them, that her talent far outstripped the dull mediocrity of theirs, that she was the only one who had inherited the full measure of their mother's talent. She brushed aside the twins' existing success, Mirry's talent, and William's intelligence, but even as she thought of them her hands balled into tight fists and the expression on her face became tainted with the bitterness of her thoughts.

The man watching her angled his spine more comfortably against the cold pillar. A dangerous, vindictive woman, and under all her sophistication perhaps a vulnerable, insecure child. His own vulnerability made him grimace a little.

He knew all about her. He knew exactly what she was doing here. He even knew about the arrangements she had made for later in the evening, but then, why shouldn't he? She was only running true to course.

He watched as she skilfully made her way round the room, creating maximum impact, arriving at John Cassavar's table just as dinner was about to be served.

He smiled to himself as she sat down, mentally applauding her aplomb and wondering if she had spared the slightest thought for the person whose seat she had taken.

Lucilla hadn't. It had been even more easy than she had expected, and now here she was, sitting at John Cassavar's table, flirting delicately with him, and lavishing on him all the praise she knew the male sex enjoyed.

She had played this role so many times . . . promising rewards with her eyes and body, echoing the ancient system of exchange and barter which had operated between the sexes throughout history.

She knew all about the reputation she had, but she didn't care. She wasn't the only actress who had slept her way to the top. Only she wasn't at the top yet, and . . . Her mask slipped momentarily and the man watching her frowned. What had caused that look of vulnerability and fear? It didn't match up with what he had been told about her. He looked at his watch . . . How much more of this farce was he going to have to endure? Amusement had given way to a desire for the whole thing to be over; it was lingering like an acid taste in the mouth. He straightened up from the pillar, a tall man, well over six feet, lithely built with an indolent way of moving that automatically drew female eyes.

He had had his share of sexual experience over the years, but he was fastidious in his tastes, with no desire to gorge himself to the point of satiation on purely physical desire. His last relationship had been with a woman who had wanted to marry him, but he hadn't felt able to give her the commitment he felt necessary for marriage and so they had parted, and now she was married to someone else. That had been over twelve months ago, and tonight, watching

Lucilla parade her bag of tricks, he had been aroused in spite of all that he knew. He was sufficiently experienced and sophisticated to be amused. She was not even really his type. He preferred brunettes. Blondes were too obvious, even when they were genuine.

Cleverly, one by one Lucilla excluded the others at the table from the conversation. She was too skilled to talk about the soap, but of course both she and John Cassavar knew why she was here.

This was the first time they had met, but she had already written to him suggesting herelf for the role, and she had seen that he recognised her name when she introduced herself. But then, so he should; it was an extremely illustrious one in the profession, and she had taken it for her own with a cynical disregard for the fact that it was not legally hers. Whoever had heard of Malcolm Chalmers?

Whoever in the profession would recognise her real father's name? And besides, she had every right to call herself Bellaire. Her stepfather had preferred *her* to any of his natural children . . . especially his eldest daughter Beatrice. Lucilla smiled secretly to herself, relishing the memory of the times she had deliberately put Beatrice down and made her step-father laugh at his eldest child's lack of grace and talent.

She felt no compunction about what she had done. Life was a challenge and she intended to win, and besides . . . Her face darkened slightly as she remembered the grudge she held against Beatrice; but John Cassavar was saying something to her . . .

something about leaving the party early.

Her heart leapt. This was what she had been hoping for. Despite her outward control, her palms felt clammy. It didn't matter how often she did this, there was still that same feeling of sick fear beforehand, and yet, what could go wrong? She had perfected it to the point where nothing *could* go wrong.

When John Cassavar went to his hotel room she would be there waiting for him. He would make a play of resisting her . . . they always did, but then . . .

She would wait until he was at his most vulnerable before delivering the blow . . . She shivered a little at the memory of those other times . . . once or twice she had actually felt physical fear, but she had always won, and she always would.

Unless he gave her the part, she would accuse him of rape. The publicity would destroy him, of course, and he would have to give in.

It had worked before, but this was the first time she had played for such high stakes. In the past she had been discreet. Small roles . . . nothing too ambitious . . . roles which had brought her to the attention of important eyes and which should have led to better things, but which somehow never had.

But this time it would be different. This time . . .

She had no moral scruples about what she was doing, or about the reputation she had gained; she cared nothing for the reproachful looks Beatrice gave her every time her name appeared in a salacious gossip column item.

Her eyes burned recklessly, betraying her

thoughts. If someone had told her that she was the victim of a deep psychological schism within herself she would have laughed at them. She was simply doing what women had always done: using her natural talent to secure what she wanted, After all, it was not her fault but theirs for not automatically recognising her talent.

She could already feel the crisp thickness of the contract in her hands . . . could almost see the headlines proclaiming her to be a new star . . . *the* new star. She could hardly wait to tell Beatrice and the others. She would go down to the Cotswolds for the weekend.

John Cassavar was looking at his watch. That was her cue. Gracefully excusing herself, she stood up and said her goodbyes.

The man watching her from the other side of the room grimaced to himself as he watched her skilfully making her way to one of the exits.

So be it. He put down his empty glass and followed her . . .

It hadn't been difficult to obtain a key for John Cassavar's suite; after all, she had done this sort of thing often enough before. A quick visit to one of the hotel's elegant cloakrooms first to remove her underwear—after all, it had worked for Marilyn Monroe, she reflected cynically, refusing to consider the price the blonde star had had to pay for her success.

It was always at this point that the danger of what she was doing hit her, that her threatened accusation could end up being based on fact. But she always chose men who had too much to lose to risk being threatened with rape; and after all, she was not just some little nobody of a would-be starlet . . . she had the security of her family name behind her. And there had never been a time when she had not escaped unscathed in the end.

The suite was in darkness, which surprised her. Had John Cassavar gone to bed already?

She closed the outer door silently, and waited until her eyes had adjusted to the darkness before making any move. She didn't want to risk switching on any lights at this stage.

The oval sitting-room was quite large, with several doors off it. One of them was open, she could see the shadowy outline of the bed inside it and she started to walk toward it.

Half-way there, she stopped. The feeling that came over her was so familiar that she didn't need to question it. It didn't matter how often she told herself that she didn't care what she had to do to succeed, there always came this moment when she suffered fear and self-hatred, and most of all a bitter anguish that it should be necessary. She had the Bellaire looks and the Bellaire talent, so why weren't they enough?

She drew a shaky breath and then walked determinedly into the bedroom.

The door closed sharply behind her and she spun round, blinded momentarily by the unexpected flash of light as someone flicked the switch.

'Walk into my parlour, said the spider to the fly . . .' she heard a mocking male voice exclaim, and her heart started thumping quickly with shock as she stared into the unexpected face of the man who had been watching her in the ballroom.

Closer to, he looked far less indolent than she remembered, and far more powerful. Her stomach muscles cramped and she had to fight the temptation to run for the door.

'Who the hell are you?' she demanded challengingly. Attack was always the best means of defence.

'I could ask you the same question,' he told her wryly. He was looking at her in a way that no man other than her half-brother Elliot had ever looked at her, with something between amusement and contempt. It made her colour angrily.

'Look, I don't know what's going on here.' she tried to bluff. 'This is John Cassavar's suite. He asked me to meet him up here.'

To her fury, her adversary merely laughed.

'Nice try,' he complimented her. 'But it won't work. John would run a mile rather than get entangled with a she-wolf like you. You see, I do know . . . or at least I know what you *planned* would be going on.' Iron had entered his voice, and to her chagrin Lucilla found herself instinctively edging back from him.

His eyes, she noticed, were a piercingly sharp shade of ice-grey that actually made her feel as though the temperature in the room had suddenly dropped.

'I must say I have to admire your aplomb,' he added mockingly. 'Not to mention your overabundance of *chutzpah*. You do know, don't you, that my brother-in-law is famous, or should I say *notorious* for his fidelity?'

John Cassavar was his brother-in-law! Lucilla's eyes narrowed and glittered like a cornered cat's, her mouth thinning and drawing back slightly over even little teeth. She longed to claw savagely at the undeniably handsome and infuriatingly complacent male face in front of her. Echoes of her childhood, when her peers' laughter had sometimes driven her to a frenzy of inner rage, made her burn to destroy him for daring to mock her, but there was nothing she could do. Nothing he would allow her to do, she recognised, and as for his comment about John Cassavar being married . . . She had known, or at least she had heard, but she had chosen to dismiss that knowledge.

'John also has a horror of scenes, especially those thrown by ambitious and unscrupulous young women. I've been watching you all evening, and I must say I have to admire your skill. Of course, we were prewarned about what to expect. Nevertheless, I derived a considerable amount of amusement from watching you.'

His voice actually lifted a little, as though he were reliving that amusement, but Lucilla paid no attention. She was too busy thinking about something else—something more important.

Prewarned . . . A chill of sensation touched her spine, dancing icy fingers tauntingly along it. No one had known what she intended to do, unless . . . unless John Cassavar had been tipped off by one of her previous victims. Goose-bumps actually lifted under her skin. None of them would surely have dared to tell the truth, to admit how she had tricked them? She mentally reviewed the men concerned; all of them proud of their reputations as males of great sexual prowess.

'Who told you?' she demanded bitterly.

His eyebrows lifted as much in amusement as anything else, she recognised.

'Why, you did,' he told her calmly. 'When you stole my ticket.'

'Your ticket . . .'

She couldn't help it. Her eyes rounded in lack of comprehension.

'Well, shall we say that when poor Matty discovered that she had allowed you to have a ticket you had no right to, she was so upset and flustered about what Max would say that I volunteered to give her mine. Max isn't very pleased with you, you know.'

'Max can go to hell,' Lucilla told him inelegantly. 'I don't give a damn. I'm right for this part. I know I am . . .'

She forgot that he was her adversary as her whole body tensed eagerly with the burning need of her ambition.

It was like a shock of cold water to hear him saying dispassionately, 'No, you're not. You're at least ten years too old, for one thing . . . For another, you're far too brittle, and for a third . . .' He looked at her thoughtfully and then said quietly, 'For a third, you just don't have the talent.'

Silence . . . She had heard those words many,

many times before, but never said in that quiet,
reflective tone of voice that was completely without
any shade of emotional reaction. Impossible to tell
from that voice alone whether, like those others, he
was loving telling her or loathing it.

She had first heard them at drama school,
expressed diffidently and then impatiently as she
had persisted in refusing to accept them. She did
have the talent . . . she had to have it. Inheriting it
was what she had based her whole life on. Hearing
those words in that cool, remote voice was like
standing there and watching someone rip her soul
out of her body. She wanted to weep great tears of
blood and pain, to scream at him that he was wrong,
that she knew he was wrong, that he *had* to be
wrong.

'Hard to take, isn't it? But believe me, once you
accept it and stop behaving like a spoiled child,
you'll be a much happier person . . .'

The gall of the man! For a moment she was too
furious to speak. When she did, her voice had lost its
normal smoothness, and it sounded rough and sore
. . . like her throat.

'Thanks for the psychoanalysis . . .'

He cut her off before she could give vent to her
bitter thoughts. 'I've been there myself. You're born
into one of the world's greatest acting families; you
grow up thinking you're automatically going to
follow in their footsteps, and for a while everyone
else thinks so too. And then slowly others begin to
see what you can't . . . that you haven't inherited
that vital ingredient . . . that special spark . . .'

'No . . .' Lucilla could hear the panic in her voice. 'No, I *have* inherited it . . .'

She had based her whole life on the premise that she had inherited her mother's acting ability; she couldn't simply turn her back on all those years of dreams and plans, and certainly not on the say-so of this one arrogant man.

But what about all the others who had gone before? The people who had given her parts . . . introductions . . . who had at first been eager to help the daughter of Cressida Bellaire, and who had eventually lost interest, turned their backs.

She could feel the familiar sense of panic swelling inside her. Another few minutes and she would be gasping for air, panicking that she was not going to be able to breathe. Oh, God, that was all she needed—that this man should see her in the grip of one of those debilitating, shaming attacks—which only came in her dreams these days.

She willed herself not to lose control, her long painted fingernails digging into the soft, well-cared-for skin of her palms as she fought down the panic.

The attacks were a legacy from something that had happened to her a long time ago. Something she couldn't think about even now without breaking out into a shivering sweat that could, at its worst, develop into a full-blown attack of acute panic that usually ended with her curled up into a protective foetus-type ball of locked muscles. But she mustn't think about that now, mustn't allow herself to remember the darkness of that claustrophobic cupboard . . . the fear that she was going to be locked away there for ever . . . She mustn't remember that now.

Through the gathering waves of panic she heard the even, male voice saying something, and she clung despairingly to its sound; at first no more than an oddly comforting echo, and then, as the fear slipped away, the echo resolved itself into recognisable sounds that she found herself paying attention to.

'You have absolutely no chance of conning John into giving you that part,' he was telling her bluntly.

'And he sent you here to tell me that, did he?' she threw at him.

She didn't care what she said—anything, anything at all as long as it kept the nightmare at bay . . .

'Not exactly. After all, we could have been wrong . . . but we weren't, were we? And I was curious to see the woman who thought she could seduce a man away from my sister . . .' He saw her face and asked grimly, 'Have you ever met my sister, Lucilla?'

'No,' she told him shortly. But she knew all about the fabled American actress who was married to John Cassavar. Her mother had been equally famous; her father a well-known director and later part-owner of one of the famous Hollywood studios; her grandparents on both sides also involved in the Hollywood scene . . . And this man was her brother.

'Ah, now there is an actress.' His eyes gleamed, whether with malice or amusement she couldn't say. She felt drained to the point of total exhaustion; something which always followed these attacks. 'I must arrange for you to meet her some time . . .'

'You won't be arranging anything in my life,' Lucilla told him shortly. 'I'm leaving.'

'What . . . already? How disappointing. You have a most intriguing reputation, you know. A very impressive list of past . . . er . . . mentors.'

Lucilla saw the way he was looking at her and was terrified—and it showed.

Up until then he had been mildly chagrined by the fact that he found her desirable, but when he saw the look of fear cross her fact his chagrin gave way to something else—something all his instincts warned him was dangerous. Of all the women he had known, why should it be this one who caught at his heart-strings like this? It was so very much at odds with her reputation, and it wasn't feigned.

He had spoken the truth when he had told her that she had not inherited any acting ability; that look of terrified loathing would have sent Hitchcock into ecstasy and it couldn't be manufactured. So what had caused it? His laconic taunt?

It would have been more in keeping with her reputation if she had taken him up on it; in fact, he had half been expecting that she would . . . hoping that she would in fact, because that would have killed stone-dead this irritating frisson of desire he felt at the sight of her.

He had nothing against women who genuinely found him attractive, and made a play for him. He didn't stand in moral judgement. God knew, he had enough experience of Hollywood to know better than that, even if his step-grandfather had insisted on sending him away to school in England once he realised what Hollywood was doing to him.

He had a lot to thank his grandfather for, he recognised; without his guiding hand he could well have become the male counterpart of the woman standing in front of him. He mocked his own inclination to feel compassion for her, reminding himself that she would have destroyed his sister's marriage with no compunction at all, to satisfy her own ambition.

'What's wrong?' he asked her.

Lucilla sprang back from him instinctively, her face drawn into grim lines of revulsion. 'Don't touch me . . .'

'Thanks for the warning,' he told her, deliberately ignoring her reaction, to add, 'Let's see . . . you're twenty-eight now . . . and just going on the list that Max gave me, you must have lost your enthusiasm by now. Doesn't your way of getting to the top strike you as risky?'

She opened her mouth to tell him how wrong he was—that, far from having a long list of past lovers behind her, she would in fact have been the most cautious sexual partner he could ever find, and then abruptly she realised what she was doing.

Without a word she swung round on her heel and practically ran from the suite.

CHAPTER TWO

THE PHONE rang abruptly, mid-morning, shattering the thick silence of Lucilla's bedroom.

She had bought the place two years ago when Elliott and Beatrice had got married. Driven by her lifelong determination to outshine her half-sister, she had engaged two of London's most *outré* interior designers with the brief that they were to make the place as dramatic and striking as possible, telling them that she wanted the place to be instantly recognisable as the home of a successful actress.

The resulting torrent of colour that poured from all three bedrooms and the dining-room to converge in a vivid, not to say garish, pool of vibrant blues, hot reds, black and gold in her sitting-room sometimes reminded her of a Cecil B. de Mille setting at its worst.

She was heartily sick and tired of the innovative ideas of her chosen designers, who seemed to think that tacking up a few yards of gaudy fabric and charging an exorbitant price for it was all there was to interior designing, and in her lowest moments Lucilla was forced to admit that she was not surprised that they had since returned to the ranks of the great unknown from which they had sprung with a fanfare of glossy magazine articles following their decoration of a leading cult singer's home.

In contrast, Beatrice's Cotswold home with its mellow polished wood and soft pretty chintzes was everything that an English country house ought to be, and with the sound of the telephone ringing demandingly in her ear, Lucilla winced at the unpleasantness of peacock blue walls and a dark red ceiling and the effect it was having on her aching head.

She picked up the receiver reluctantly.

'Miss Bellaire, it's the Howard Agency here . . . We've arranged an audition for you for this afternoon.'

The crisp female voice wasn't Matty's, but Lucilla was too tense to question why.

Perhaps John Cassavar had changed his mind. Perhaps he was going to let her audition, after all. She gripped the receiver tightly, but the name she was given wasn't John Cassavar's, after all, but someone she had never heard of, at an obscure address in the West End.

Without bothering to thank the girl, she replaced the receiver.

What was the audition for? She hadn't been told. She shrugged. What did it matter? It was work. Another chance to prove to the world that she was worthy of the Bellaire name.

God, she hoped the role was a good one, then she could show that arrogant, stupid brother-in-law of John Cassavar's just how wrong he was about her. How dared he tell her that she had no talent?

But if she had, why at the age of twenty-eight was she still searching for a major role to thrust her into the limelight?

She stopped what she was doing, putting down her make-up brush, ignoring her reflection. Soul-searching wasn't something she normally indulged in; although quick to see the vulnerabilities of others, she preferred to see herself as being completely without them.

She switched her attention back at her face. She was twenty-eight year old and, though still a beautiful woman, she lacked the freshness of an eighteen-year-old; she shivered, trying to shake off the feeling that the hand of fate had passed over her . . . that for her there was never going to be that mind-drugging moment when she knew that she only had to reach out and she would be there, her reputation and status surpassing even that of her mother.

It *was* going to happen. It had to . . . She had just been unlucky. And then, reluctantly, she remembered what Elliott had said to her at Christmas.

She had gone to the Cotswolds unwillingly, having refused the only role Max had been able to find for her . . . something in a provincial panto that she had curled her mouth at.

Elliott had taken her on one side on Christmas Day while everyone else was enthusing over their presents. Beatrice, idiot that she was, and despite the way they had once treated her, still liked to surround herself with her family.

'Give it up, Lulu,' Elliott had told her, surprising her by reverting to his childhood name for her. 'If you aren't tired of destroying yourself by endlessly attempting to be something you aren't, then at least have pity on those of us who are tired of watching you.

Look at yourself . . . There must be something better in life for you than forever chasing after something that doesn't exist, that *can't* exist for you.'

She had pretended not to understand him, and had deliberately avoided meeting his eyes for the rest of the day, leaving earlier than she had planned, despite Beatrice's concern.

If she could be content to be like Beatrice—able to accept that although she was a Bellaire by name she was not by nature . . . If she were able to settle for a life that encompassed a husband and family . . . But she wasn't, she wanted more—she needed more excitement, challenge. Only when she reached the peak of her profession would she be safe, invulnerable . . .

Perhaps then the nightmares might stop.

'Don't think about it,' she told herself quickly. She was tense enough at the thought of the audition, without adding that.

It came to her then that, whereas she ought to be excited and pleasurably nervous at the thought of going for the audition, in actual fact she was sick with fear and dread. What was happening to her? She was allowing other people's judgements to affect her own. Just because one man, and a stranger at that, who didn't really know her, had told her she couldn't act . . . that was no reason to throw her off balance like this. Unless of course he was only confirming what she herself already knew.

Her hand was shaking so much that she had to put down the brush. Through the mirror, her own eyes looked back at her frozen with fear.

Oh, God, she couldn't go on like this!

She took a taxi to the audition, grimacing at the seedy building outside which she was dropped.

There were no names to say who occupied the offices, and she paused to check the address again before going inside.

A clumsily drawn arrow pointed upwards and said 'Reception'.

She had to walk up two flights of stone steps to find it, and she wrinkled her nose as the stale smell of fast food and cheap perfume gushed out when she opened the frosted glass door.

A brunette with a punk hairdo and long black nails sat behind the desk, chewing gum and reading a magazine.

Lucilla gave her name disdainfully. In many ways it was no worse than some of the provincial repertory theatres she had played in, and yet there was something about the whole set-up that made her skin prickle warningly.

'You can go in,' the girl told her in a bored voice, having first checked a list on her desk. 'Through this door and then first right.'

She jerked her head in the direction of the door behind her.

It opened into a blank corridor with several doors off it. All of them were closed, and Lucilla tapped on the first on the right and then pushed it open.

Three men occupied the room; one of them sitting behind a cheap plastic desk, the two others standing up.

All three of them looked at her as she walked in— brutal, assessing looks that reduced her body to a piece of saleable flesh and made her scalp crawl with revulsion.

'All right, strip off . . . and then go and lie on there,' the man behind the desk told her uninterestedly. Ignoring Lucilla's frozen rage, he turned to his companions and said tiredly, 'I've told Guy before not to send me anyone over twenty-one. They always look like dogs on film, and besides, the punters like 'em young and fresh . . . Gives 'em an added thrill . . .'

He suddenly realised that Lucilla hadn't moved and he turned to her and said disagreeably, 'OK, girlie, get moving. We haven't got all day . . .'

Max had sent her to audition for a blue film, Lucilla suddenly recognised sickly. How could he? He knew exactly how she felt about skin-flicks . . . She started to shake with rage. What on earth was he trying to do to her? She didn't even know he handled this kind of stuff . . . In fact, she was sure he didn't. This kind of thing, this grimy, twilight side of the profession, had its own agencies, its own experts . . . and heaven help the straight actress who was ever found to have tried to promote her early career in the pornographic industry.

Lucilla had always steered clear of anything of that nature. She detested the thought of baring her body for the lustful delectation of the people who bought such things; in fact, she loathed the very idea of appearing in anything remotely sexually orientated. And Max knew it.

Without saying a word she swept toward the door, banging it violently behind her. In the outer office she stopped only to glare at the girl behind the desk before speedily leaving the building.

She ought to have known . . . she ought to have

guessed from the very appearance of the place, she seethed as she looked for another taxi. God, and to think she'd had the naïve idea that because of the money to be made in such filth that it was all conducted in luxurious surroundings. She had thought it was only the straight side of the business that had to make do with run-down offices in buildings that looked as though they were about to be condemned.

It took her ten minutes to find a cab, and she saw from the way the driver looked at her that he thought he knew exactly what kind of business it was that took her to Max's offices. For the first time in her adult life she was glad that she wasn't famous.

She was still seething when she marched past the commissionaire who guarded the entrance to Max's hi-tech glass and chrome offices.

He knew her well, but he had never seen her looking the way she did today, he reflected. Normally she looked like ice. Beautiful ice, but still ice. Today . . . Well, today, for the first time that he could remember, he had actually found himself fancying her.

Grinning to himself, he wondered what was going to happen when she walked into Max's office.

There was no familiar Matty sitting behind her desk, surrounded by untidy piles of paper, but instead, a chic girl several years her own junior, wearing what to Lucilla's affronted eyes was an obviously far more expensive and fashionable outfit than her own.

How on earth did a girl working for the appalling wages she knew Max paid manage to afford to wear Giorgio Armani? There was only one way . . . She glared at the girl as she stormed past her, heading for

Max's door, and was astounded to hear her saying coolly, 'I'm sorry. I'm afraid you can't go in there . . .'

Lucilla turned on her, ready to tell her that nobody, but nobody stopped her from doing exactly what she wanted to do, when the office door opened and from behind her a cool, and definitely familiar, and oh, so definitely amused male voice announced, 'I'll deal with this, Charlotte.'

She whirled round, and exclaimed in goaded accents, 'Oh, my God, you! I might have known. Where's Max? And what the hell are you doing here? Or has your brother-in-law sent *you* out to find him a suitable actress to play Tabitha St Alban?'

'Which question shall I answer first?' he asked her, patently unperturbed by her anger. Somehow or other she found herself inside Max's office with the door closed very firmly.

'I want to see Max,' Lucilla said firmly.

His mouth twitched and she wanted to hit him. Something seemed to be pleasing him very much; he looked like a man who'd gambled on the strength of an extremely speculative hunch, and not only won, but won with the odds very much in his favour.

'You do? Then I suggest you book yourself a flight to St Andrews. He's playing golf,' he elucidated, smiling at her.

Lucilla felt herself swell with frustrated rage.

'Then he'd better damn well stop playing golf and get himself back here! I want to know what the hell he's playing at . . . sending me to audition for . . .' She broke off, two dark spots of colour burning her cheeks.

'For . . . ?' he prompted, leaning his weight on the

edge of Max's desk and folding his arms.

'I'm sorry to interrupt you, Mr Barrington, but the Press are on the phone, wanting to know if it's true that you've taken over the agency from Mr Goldberg.'

The cool, well-modulated tones of the receptionist reached Lucilla quite clearly, as the intercom chirruped, and he reached over the desk to flick it on.

She scarcely heard his reply, too stunned by the information that Max was no longer in charge of the agency. Max *was* the agency. He had started it when her mother and stepfather were still in their late teens. They had been among his first clients.

She sat down and stared at him.

'Do you know that's the first inelegant movement I've seen you make . . .' He watched as her eyes focused on him, their shock sharpening to icy dislike. He knew exactly why she was here . . . He had taken a million to one chance, determined to prove something to himself, and he had been right, dammit! Against all the odds, he had been right . . . He wasn't quite sure how it had happened, but this angry, beautiful woman standing in front of him, whose reputation was that of someone who would go to bed with anyone who would offer her a part, was as ignorant of sexual intimacy as a Vestal virgin. Although it was a bad comparison, because they hadn't been virginal at all, come to think of it. But *she* was . . . he was sure of it.

He hardly knew her, and yet already she had aroused within him physical desire, anger, impatience, irritation, dislike. And at the same time he had felt for her an almost overwhelming compassion, a sense of shared unhappiness and confusion, a feeling that he knew her innermost vulnerabilities as intimately as he knew his own. He had conquered his, but he was intensely aware that without his grandfather to support him he could well be like her: bitter, frustrated, desperately lonely, relentlessly seeking something that could never be found.

That was the inheritance she had been given by her mother, he thought grimly, and he knew exactly how cruelly heavy that burden could be.

'Barrington,' Lucilla repeated huskily, her forehead pleating in a frown as she searched her memory for the elusive connection. And then she remembered it and her eyes widened in recognition. He saw the recognition and wondered wryly to himself how he could ever have thought her vulnerable.

'You're one of the Hollywood Barringtons.'

'Nick Barrington,' he confirmed drily.

God, she ought to have realised when he said he was John Cassavar's brother-in-law. Everyone knew that John Cassavar had married into one of Hollywood's most famous families; a family that embraced every single aspect of the film world; a family that in each and every generation had produced equally famous shining stars. He looked nothing like his famous sister, or his parents.

He saw her expression and knew what she was thinking. Let her keep on guessing. Sooner or later she would probably find out about the gossip. It didn't bother him now and his parents were both dead, so there was no one left to be hurt by the old rumours. And what did they matter, anyway? God, his mother wasn't the only woman in the world to be unfaithful to her marriage vows. It had been hard, though, as a teenager, coming to realise just why he was the subject of so much speculation.

'*You've* taken over the agency?'

'Not exactly. I'm an accountant, not an agent. I work for the company which has bought Max out.'

He didn't bother to tell her that he was that company; that, having accepted that he had no acting flair, he had instead developed the talent he did have.

Lucilla stood up slowly and grabbed the end of the desk. She was only three feet away from him, her eyes glittering with malevolence and rage.

'So it was *you* who sent me for that audition, wasn't it?'

'Didn't you get it?' he asked her innocently. 'I thought it would be right up your street.'

She would have hit him then, but she was too aware of how easily those lean brown hands could circle her wrists and hold her prisoner . . . of how frightening it would be to be so close to him.

'I never audition for . . . for that kind of filth,' she spat at him. 'Max knows that . . .'

Suddenly her anger left her. She felt weak and shaky, close to tears almost; something totally alien to her. She never cried—hadn't cried, in fact, since her mother had told her it made her look ugly. In those days she had thought her mother resented her, and she had done everything she could to win her approval. It was only later that she realised that it was her father Cressida resented . . . because he was not Charles.

She realised that since Nick Barrington must have already discussed her with Max to have known that she would seek out his brother-in-law, he most probably knew exactly how she felt about the porn films. She said tightly, 'I suppose this is your idea of revenge?'

'If I wanted revenge, I can think of a hundred better ways to get it than that. No, it was more in the light of an experiment,' he told her. He got up, and for a moment she thought he was actually going to touch her. He watched as she shrank back, torn between amusement and pity, and then said quietly, 'Lucilla, I don't want you to look on me in the light of a persecutor—that's not my role at all.'

'Then what is?' she demanded bitterly.

He turned his back to her, and she could have sworn she heard him saying the word 'Saviour', but before she could challenge him on his arrogance he turned to face her and told her, 'Let's just say that I'm a man looking for a cause, and you could well be it.'

The meaning of the obscure words defeated her. He was obviously playing some kind of game with her. Well, he could go on playing it on his own. She had had enough.

'Since Max is no longer in charge, I'm going to find myself another agent,' she told him freezingly, preparing to sweep out.

His infuriatingly calm, 'Do you think you can?' stopped her.

She opened her mouth to tell him that any number of agents would be only too pleased to have her on their books, and then remembered that only at Christmas she had mentioned to Seb that she thought Max was getting past it and that she might switch to his agent, and he had told her dampeningly, 'I shouldn't if I were you.' He had even dared to suggest that Max kept her on as a client because of his sentimental attachment to the memories of his most famous clients of all, her mother and stepfather.

'Second thoughts? Good. You see, I think I know how your unique talent can best be put to use.'

Lucilla stared suspiciously at him. She was sure he was laughing at her, but she couldn't resist the temptation.

'How?'

'I want you to come and work here at the agency. To take charge . . .'

Lucilla stared at him.

'Me, take Max's place?'

'Yes. You can do it,' he told her encouragingly. 'You've got the contacts and the know-how . . . You've got the determination.'

He reached out and touched her face before she could move out of the way, cupping it with surprisingly gentle fingers . . . the kind of touch that would soothe the most tender bruise, she found herself thinking as she stared in bemused shock into his eyes without even trying to move away.

'You might not have any talent as an actress, Lucilla, but I think you do have the ability to discern that skill in others. Stop tearing yourself apart reaching out for something you can never have, and use the talent you do have.'

An agent instead of an actress? Never!

'No,' she told him baldly, twitching her head beyond his touch. 'Never.'

'I'll give you a week to think about it,' he responded, totally ignoring her refusal, and producing a thick, plain business card.

'Here's my private number . . . You see how much I want you,' he added wickedly.

She glowered at him, but when she reached home she discovered that she had actually picked up the card, and, instead of destroying it as she had intended, she found herself slipping it into her address book.

Old habits, she told herself. You soon learned in the acting profession to use everything and everyone.

The phone rang as she stood beside it. At first she stared at it, thinking it would be Nick, but then she picked it up.

'Lucilla, it's me, Bea. Can you make it next weekend? Everyone else is coming. It's Elliott's birthday.'

She wanted to refuse, but instead she heard herself saying grudgingly, 'All right, although God knows why someone of Elliott's age should want to celebrate the addition of another year.'

CHAPTER THREE

THERE was no viable reason why she shouldn't go to Elliott's birthday party. It was true that she was due to begin rehearsals for the very small part Max had obtained for her in a fringe theatre play which its writer was hoping to take to the Edinburgh Festival next year. It was the kind of play that 'developed in tune with the actors' perceptions of their roles'.

Lucilla had told Max that she had no intention of contributing anything to any writer's perceptions, claiming that 'to do so was to write the damn play for him'.

She had a second reason for accepting Beatrice's invitation, though she was reluctant to acknowledge it.

Nicholas Barrington had given her a week to make up her mind about his ridiculous suggestion that she work for him as his assistant. Work as a mere agent's assistant—it was ludicrous that he should even think of it. Being conveniently away at the weekend when he would try to get in touch with her to get her answer would let him know exactly how she felt about the idea.

She tossed her head arrogantly and looked in the mirror. In her bedroom, with the morning light shimmering in through the closed curtains, her skin looked translucent and as fine as a child's, the tiny lines that were already beginning to form at the corners of her eyes unnoticeable. Here in this light she could quite easily have passed for seventeen . . . Well, almost. She still hadn't given up on getting the coveted 'soap' role. There had to be a way and she would find that way . . . somehow.

She was having lunch at Le Gavroche, one of the Princess of Wales' favourite lunch-time haunts. The very sizeable trust fund left to her by her father meant that she could indulge herself in a good many of life's luxuries.

Her affluence was resented by several of her acquaintances, struggling actresses and actors whose acid comments Lucilla put down to the fact that she possessed the famous Bellaire name and they did not.

The two women she was lunching with today were probably her closest friends; one of them played the central female role in a TV series and the other had given up her ambitions of finding stardom and had settled instead for marriage to an extremely wealthy industrialist.

They were her closest friends; they met every Tuesday lunch time at Le Gavroche, and yet Lucilla knew there was no way she was going to tell them about what had happened with Nicholas Barrington, nor about his snide comments concerning her lack of acting talent.

In the past she would simply have congratulated herself on her astuteness in not betraying any weakness of vulnerability to others, but today for some reason she found herself wishing she was more like Bea, more able to open herself up to others and seek their advice.

Advice? What did she need advice for? She already

knew what she was going to do. What did she need to even waste time on Nicholas Barrington's idiotic suggestion for? She already knew where her future lay. He was probably only doing it so that he could get her into bed, anyway. Lucilla was so used to men desiring her that she automatically took it for granted that they all did.

But Nicholas Barrington had had ample opportunity to make a play for her that night in his brother-in-law's hotel suite, and he had done nothing. She got up from her seat in front of her dressing-table. She didn't want to think about that night, and she wasn't going to.

She arrived late for lunch, sweeping into the restaurant wearing a black wool crêpe suit with a short, straight skirt that revealed the stunning length of her legs, and a jacket cut like a military cape and trimmed with sable on the cuffs and collar.

Le Gavroche wasn't the sort of place where the female diners ever allowed themselves to be stunned by the outfits worn by other women, but Lucilla had the satisfaction of sensing the brief hiatus her appearance caused.

It was enough, and she smiled benignly at the waiter as he rushed to escort her to her table.

Her friends were already there. Samantha Lewis, bored with her industrialist and still tiresomely plump after the arrival of her second child raised her eyebrows and enquired sweetly, 'Sable? My dear, the anti-fur brigade won't like that.'

And Helen Masters, not quire as secure in her TV role as she would have liked to have been, added acidly, 'You're so lucky to have independent means, Lucilla. After all, let's face it, darling, on what you earn you wouldn't be able to afford so much as the price of a cup of coffee in here.'

Lucilla felt their envious resentment, and normally it was like a charge of adrenalin to her, reinforcing her own belief that she was superior . . . that she was special. Today, though, for some reason it just depressed her, and when she made no comment Helen added tauntingly, 'I believe you were at the Grosvenor the other night. Has John offered you anything in his new soap? They're casting the smaller parts first, I believe. The mother of the heroine . . . that sort of thing. That would be a good role for you, darling . . .'

Lucilla didn't retaliate. In fact, she hardly heard the insult because the moment Helen mentioned John Cassavar she felt as though she was back in Nicholas Barrington's office, hearing him tell her that there was no way she would ever make a successful actress. A tiny shiver of sensation rushed across her skin; an awareness that she had reached a turning point in her life.

'Look, isn't that Tracy Hammond?' Samantha hissed, and all three of them turned to look discreetly at the small blonde girl who, together with her entourage, was standing by the entrance.

'Eighteen, and already she's got her pick of roles to choose from. How on earth does she do it? She's nothing special to look at,' Samantha said pettishly. 'Heavens, any one of us could outshine her in that department, even now.'

It was true, and yet the girl had something, Lucilla

acknowledged, watching the small, mobile face as the young actress talked to the people with her. That smile . . . those delicate arching eyebrows . . . those shadows of light and dark that played across her face. Yes, she would be the perfect instrument for conveying emotions . . .

Lucilla shivered, feeling abruptly as though someone had walked over grave. What was it Nicholas had said to her . . . ?

Was he some kind of sorcerer who, simply by putting the thought into her mind, had turned her into what he wanted? Just for a moment she had actually found herself visualising Tracy Hammond in the role she had wanted for herself . . . had visualised it and seen the rightness of the girl doing it. But that was impossible, of course. Even if she were to take the job. Even if Nicholas Barrington should agree that Tracy was right for the role, she happened to know that Tracy Hammond was already committed to film work that would be taking her out of the country for the best part of the next eight months.

And the reason she knew was standing just behind the young actress, smiling mockingly in Lucilla's direction as he caught her eye.

'Heavens, isn't that one of your brothers with her?' Helen enquired, spotting Benedict's blond head.

'Half-brothers,' Lucilla corrected her, watching as Benedict expertly detached both himself and Tracy from the others and came over to her table.

'Good heavens, Lulu, it is you, after all. For a moment you looked so like Mother that I was . . .'

Lucilla didn't make the mistake of thinking she had

been paid a compliment.

She and Benedict had never got on. Of the two of them she preferred his twin, Sebastian, who was quieter, less sharply abrasive and relentlessly acerbic. She and Benedict had always sat on two opposite sides of the family fence. Benedict adored his elder sister Beatrice; or at least he adored her as much as his intensely selfish nature would allow, whereas Lucilla hated her.

The reason for that hatred was deeply buried in their shared childhood. She had never spoken to anyone about it; terrified to do so because even to think about it was to release her private monster from its cage, like springing the lid off a jack in the box.

When Lucilla made no response to his taunt, Benedict added magnanimously, 'It must be the light in here, or perhaps it's that outfit . . . black can be so draining when one gets older. Tracy, now . . . well, she looks stunning in it,' he added wickedly.

The younger actress raised her eyebrows, plainly not the slightest bit impressed by his flattery, and, virtually ignoring Benedict, said calmly to Lucilla, 'I think I saw you the other night at the party for John Cassavar. You were standing quite close to Nicholas Barrington, that's why I noticed you.'

She gave Lucilla a smile to show that her remark was not intended to be offensive.

'I particularly noticed the way he was watching you, and felt quite envious. He's gorgeous, isn't he? I believe he's taken over a London theatrical agency. I heard it on the grapevine.'

Lucilla saw that Benedict was frowning slightly.

'Who is he? I've never heard of him.'

'You will!' Tracy assured him. 'He's got a reputation for being a marvellous person to do business with, although he doesn't usually work as an agent. I think he's normally involved in far more behind the scenes stuff . . . finding finance for films, that kind of thing.'

'A glorified accountant, you mean?' Benedict commented.

'Don't sneer, Ben,' Tracy told him sharply. 'Without the money to finance them no film would ever be made, no play ever put on stage, and Nick Barrington has the reputation of being scrupulously honest and fair with everyone he deals with. Definitely a man to have on your side.'

'I know these Hollywood agents,' Benedict interrupted her. 'It's all percentages and wheeling and dealing with casting couch benefits thrown in as a bonus.'

'Not where Nick Barrington is concerned,' Tracy told him quickly. 'He isn't that sort at all.'

'You seem to know a lot about him, for someone you've never met.'

'Word gets around,' Tracy responded drily. 'All you have to do is pay attention and listen. You should try it some time, Ben.' She looked at her watch and exclaimed frantically, 'Heavens, look at the time! I must go.'

Lucilla watched them leave. Unlike the Bellaire siblings, Tracy had no theatrical background, and her first contact with the theatrical world had been a chance casting as an extra in a TV drama. The director had been so impressed with her that he had offered her a much more important role in a follow-up play, and from there her career had taken off.

Lucilla was deep in thought after Tracy and Benedict had gone. Her initial tension when Tracy had mentioned seeing her at the party had gone as she listened to the younger girl enthusing about Nick's reputation. An honest, trustworthy man who didn't give or take favours, who didn't use people and then discard them. Had he any idea how very rare that was in their world?

It was a few seconds before Lucilla realised that, instead of feeling contemptuous of him, she was actually envying him slightly.

The step from financier to agent was perhaps a rather unusual one, but Nick Barrington seemed to thrive on doing the unusual and doing it very successfully. A tiny thrill of sensation coiled through her. She could be part of that success if she chose; she could step out of one career and into another. All it needed . . .

All it needed was for her to step blindfold into the dark, she told herself acidly, and to trust that Nick would be there to catch her if she fell. And why should he? No one had performed that service for her before. She had learned young to stand on her own feet and alone. And yet there was no denying the respect and admiration with which Tracy had spoken of Nick's reputation and ability. What had she ever done that would command other people's respect? She had come here to have lunch with her friends, she reminded herself, not to think about Nicholas Barrington.

'He's stunningly good-looking, isn't he?' Helen

breathed admiringly, bringing her back down to earth.

'Who?' she demanded, frowning as she searched the room for Nick's face.

'Your brother, of course . . . Odd how the two of you have never really got on. What's his twin like?'

'Physically? Very, very similar, but Sebastian has a different personality. He's quieter . . .' Why had she thought Helen meant Nick? She was becoming dangerously obsessed by the man.

The last thing Lucilla wanted to do was to talk about the other members of her family. The day had suddenly turned sour on her; whether because Benedict had so unsubtly reminded her that the years were passing, or whether because, like it or not, she had realised when she'd looked at Tracy Hammond that Nick was right, and that the girl standing in front of her would make a perfect Tabitha, she had no idea.

For the first time that she could remember she was suddenly seeing the glitter and glamour of the life she had chosen as being faintly tawdry, faintly tarnished, and there was a sensation inside her not unlike the faint nausea that accompanied too much indulgence in rich food.

What was happening to her?

She tried to throw off her malaise, but all through lunch she was preoccupied and on edge; the chatter of her girlfriends began to grate and she found herself studying them dispassionately and wondering how on earth she had managed to endure their inanities through so many lunches.

Lucilla was very intelligent. She had been told when she was at school that she had the ability to go on to

Oxford or Cambridge, but she hadn't been interested. An academic life was not what she wanted, and yet it was true that there was a part of her that craved something deeper and more enduring than her present way of life. Perhaps that was why she got so impatient and irritated with the roles she was offered. There was so little in them . . . they were so lacking in reality . . . Take this part she was supposed to be rehearsing later in the week.

She was playing the part of a social worker in charge of a young schoolgirl heavily involved in drugs and prostitution. She had read her lines several times, and each time had been increasingly conscious of a lack of depth to them. It irritated her, as much for what she considered to be the sloppiness of the writer as for her own belief that no social worker would make the kind of inept remarks she had been given to say.

Back in her own home she read through them again. She had turned one of Elliott's original three bedrooms into an extra sitting-room off her own bedroom, and she'd had it furnished with the same kind of long, deep sofa she remembered her mother using.

Cressida, too, had had her own sitting-room—a private inner sanctum which, like her bedroom, had been sacrosanct and forbidden territory as far as her children were concerned. Lucilla had loved it, spending as much time in there as she could, sneaking in whenever she could escape from the nanny who looked after her.

Cressida had had help with all her children.

Despite giving birth to six of them, including the twins, she had always expressed distaste for babies and toddlers. All of them in turn had been restricted to the nursery until they had reached school age, and after that there had been boarding-schools, until Cressida and Charles died. Then Beatrice had given in to the pleading of her younger siblings and had allowed them to come home and attend local day-schools.

It had been ridiculous the way Beatrice had spoiled them all, and she knew that Elliott agreed with her. Witness the way he had firmly told them that, after he and Beatrice were married, he was taking his wife to live in the Cotswolds and that they could now fend for themselves. All apart from the baby of the family, William, who had still been taking his A-levels.

Now William was at Oxford, a too tall and too thin gangly creature with the fabled Bellaire blond hair and an appetite that Lucilla found frankly nauseating.

Thinking about her family reminded her that she had committed herself to spending the weekend with them. Would Benedict be there with Tracy Hammond? She closed her eyes and immediately an image of the girl dressed in clothes of the sixteenth century sprang up behind her darkened lids. Tracy would make a perfect Tabitha, there was no doubt about it.

Her eyes opened, flashing sparks of anger and resentment at her own reflection. What was wrong with her? That role was hers. Why on earth was she envisaging Tracy Hammond in it?

She was due to go to a party in the evening, but the thought held no appeal. Unusually for her, she discovered that she preferred to stay at home.

Half-way throught the evening, she switched off the video she had been watching and went over to the bookshelves to remove a couple of the dozen or so photograph albums she kept there.

They had been her mother's, and Lucilla had insisted on having them after Charles's and Cressida's deaths. Beatrice had objected, but Lucilla had overruled her.

She dared not think about the number of times she had poured over these albums. They charted her mother's and Charles's careers right from their first roles. Even during the years they had been married to different partners, Cressida had kept up the albums.

According to the critics, her mother had been one of the greatest actresses ever born. Lucilla was the image of her, everyone said so, so why at twenty-eight was she still playing minor roles . . . growing acid and despairing on her lack of success?

Hope deferred maketh the heart sick.

Lucilla shivered as the words slid into her mind, tiny poisoned barbs of truth she didn't want to acknowledge.

It was all Nicholas Barrington's fault, she thought pettishly. He was the one who was responsible for this odd malaise that seemed to be possessing her.

The phone rang and she reached for the receiver. Her bad mood was more probably induced by the garishness of her décor, she decided waspishly as she spoke into it.

'Have dinner with me.'

She recognised his voice straight away. No other man she knew possessed that underlying warmth of humour, as though something about life, and more especially her, amused him a great deal.

'I'm sorry, who's speaking?' she demanded coldly, pretending not to know him.

'Come off it, Lucilla, you know damn well who I am.'

The arrogance of the man!

'You're flattering yourself, I'm afraid,' she told him freezingly, preparing to drop the receiver back into the cradle, but he stopped her by saying calmly,

'Actually, I was flattering you. You're a trained actress, Lucilla. You ought to be able to recognise those personal nuances of tone and inflection that would be lost on others.'

She hesitated, torn between the satisfaction of continuing to pretend not to know him and denying his aspersions on her training. In the end, pride won out against caution, and she said curtly, 'I don't want to have dinner with you, Nicholas. I——'

'Not even to discuss you playing Tabitha?'

She actually felt the goose-bumps lift under her skin. Her heart seemed to miss a complete beat, a wild, spiralling sensation of excitement whirling through her. She gripped the receiver tightly and said huskily, 'Do you mean John Cassavar is actually considering me for the part?'

'No,' he told her brutally. 'I just wanted to see if

I'd managed to get through to you yet. I see I
haven't. Forget acting, Lucilla. You haven't got an
ounce of talent for it, and you know it. Stop wasting
your life pursuing impossible dreams, otherwise
you're going to end up sour and embittered. I know,
I've seen it happen.'

He wasn't even trying to be tactful. Hard upon the
heels of her shock came anger.

'It's no business of yours what the hell I do with my
life, Nicholas Barrington,' she told him curtly. 'And
as for your lousy job, you can keep it.'

As she put down the receiver, she felt an odd sense
of emptiness; a renewal of the loneliness she had
experienced at lunch time with her friends; a feeling
of being apart, of being totally alone.

She shivered. Why was she feeling like this now,
when she had deliberately chosen to be alone? Over
the years there had been any number of people,
drawn to her by her looks and her family's
reputation, who had offered her friendship and more,
but she had always rejected them, keeping them at a
distance.

Because that was what she wanted, she told herself
firmly. Success was the only companion she wanted
to share her life with.

Lucilla cursed as another taxi cruised by without
stopping. She was going to be late for the rehearsals.
Normally she wouldn't have minded, but after
yesterday's disastrous reading, when the director had
bawled her out for her, as he termed it, 'completely
lifeless' interpretation of her part, she would have

preferred not to put herself too much in the limelight.

And it was Beatrice's fault.

She had rung in the evening to say that they were having a formal dinner party for Elliott's birthday, and that meant that Lucilla had had to go out and buy a new dress. It had taken her ages to find exactly what she wanted, and now here she was, stuck in Kinghtsbridge in the pouring rain, when she ought to be right on the other side of the city.

She was almost three quarters of an hour late.

Rehearsals were being held in a riverside warehouse conversion owned by a friend of the playwright's: a vast, empty barn of a room with spectacular views and minimalistic furnishings.

Privately, Lucilla thought it too barren, although her artistic eye couldn't deny the effectiveness of the stark simplicity of white walls, black painted floorboards, chrome glass and leather furnishings.

Everyone fell silent as she walked into the room, dropping her full-length mink on to one of the chairs.

The director, a fiendishly temperamental man in his early thirties, with red hair and a milk-white complexion that turned scarlet when he was angry, rocked on to the balls of his feet and then paced toward her with feline menace.

He picked up her mink and dropped it deliberately on to the floor.

'I realise our earliest ancestors covered themselves in animal skins, darling, and bearing in mind your age I suppose we should understand your penchant for it, but please, not on Gavin's furniture.'

It was deliberate baiting, and Lucilla only just

managed to hold on to her temper. Once, she wouldn't even have bothered to try, but, much as she loathed her present role, it was the only one she had.

Visions of other scenes very similar to this one flashed through her mind; scenes during which she had given full rein to her acid tongue and its cutting sarcasm; scenes which had inevitably ended with her leaving the cast, and it struck her now that Julian was deliberately trying to provoke an argument.

She picked up the mink and slipped it back on. The room was cold enough to merit it, and said coolly, 'I'm sorry I'm late.'

'Yes, I'm sure. Knightsbridge was hell, was it?'

He looked disparagingly at the carrier she had brought in with her, but Lucilla refused to rise to the bait.

She had her script with her, and she made a great play of studying it until he turned his attention back to the scene her arrival had interrupted.

Although she didn't show it, his malice had unnerved her, and ten minutes later, when it was her turn to speak her opening lines, it showed in her inability to concentrate on them. Her concentration wasn't helped by the way Julian stood in front of her, watching her with narrowed eyes and a contemptuous smile.

He waited until she had finished, and then said acidly, 'Quite appalling, darling . . . Look, I know you aren't like the rest of us and you don't have to earn your bread and butter, but do try to put your-self in our places . . . . really, you'd be doing the whole production a favour if you simply dropped out now . . . never mind the favour you'd be doing the acting profession as a whole,' he added maliciously.

Behind her, Lucilla heard someone snigger, and she felt her face start to burn.

Julian was really into his stride now, pleasure glittering in his eyes as he saw he was getting a reaction from her.

'Let's face it, darling, you've had a damn good ten years coasting on Mama's reputation, but you haven't an ounce of talent and why on earth Equity ever agreed to give you a union card I'll never know. You do realise that you're doing someone with genuine talent out of a job, don't you? When Jeremy told me you were having this part, I warned him how it would be,' he added vituperatively. 'Let's face it, Lucilla, you can't act. You never could, and you never will.'

Somewhere in the thick silence someone coughed, a high, nervous sound, and then at the far end of the room a door opened, and the hatefully familiar voice of Nicholas Barrington called out easily, 'All right if I come in?'

Lucilla saw Julian's double-take as he saw him, his attention switching from her to Nick.

'Sorry about this, Manners,' Nick apologised easily. 'But I wanted to have a word with Lucilla . . .'

He must have followed her here, tracked her down like an eager retriever. God, did the man never give up?

Suddenly, for no understandable reason, she wanted to cry. She looked at him across the width of the room and found that her eyes actually were blurring with tears as she saw the amused kindness in his eyes.

He might almost have heard what Julian had said to her. Probably he had heard it, for the director had been speaking clearly enough for someone outside the door to catch every word. Now her humiliation was complete. No doubt Nick had enjoyed hearing someone else reinforcing what he had himself told her.

'All right, Nick,' she told him huskily. 'You win. I'll take the job.'

And, oblivious to the surprise registering on the faces of her fellow actors, she walked past Julian and up to Nick.

'It will be on my terms, though,' she warned him.

What on earth was she doing? What was she saying? Was she really relinquishing a lifetime of dreams to work for this man as his assistant? She must be dreaming. It couldn't be happening, but it was . . . Nick was already drawing her hand through his arm and escorting her towards the door.

Once there he paused, and touched the cuff of her coat consideringly.

'Lovely,' he murmured to her, so that only she could hear him. 'But it doesn't suit you. Fur coats are only for women who are prepared to take them off and make love on them.' He looked amused at the expression on her face, and added mischievously, 'Didn't you know? That's why men buy them for them.'

'I——' she told him freezingly as she opened the

door and walked through it '—bought this myself.'

'I know,' he told her, laughing at her.

What was he trying to imply? Lucilla looked at him angrily. He had trapped her, arriving like that when she was at her most vulnerable, when she wasn't expecting to see him . . . forcing her to take his job because, if she hadn't, Julian would have humiliated her in front of both him and the whole cast, by forcing her to walk out.

And without Max, whom she could coax and bully . . . Max whom she suspected had been half in love with her mother and whom she could cajole and tease into getting her auditions. How on earth would she ever manage to get another part?

It came to her then that no one director with whom she had worked had ever worked with her again. She had always known that she wasn't popular, and had put it down to jealousy on the part of others, for her illustrious background, refusing to acknowledge that Sebastian and Benedict, who shared that background, who in fact had *two* famous parents, were both popular and successful actors, while she was slowly getting smaller and smaller parts.

Her whole body felt cold, despite her fur coat. No, not her whole body; where Nick was holding her arm she felt warm. She also felt an unfamiliar urge to move closer to him. To subdue it she forced herself to concentrate on something more important.

'Why?' she asked him furiously.

'Why what?' He was all innocence.

'You know what. What were you doing? Why did

you come looking for me?'

He stopped dead in the street, forcing her to do the same, turning round so that she was pressed up against the solid bulk of his body. She put out her hands to stop herself from cannoning into him, and gasped in indignation as he took hold of them against his chest.

'You're shivering . . .' Calmly, he tucked her hands inside his unfastened jacket so that they were protected from the icy wind by its bulk and warmed by the heat of his body.

How on earth was it that she was freezing when she was wearing a fur coat, and yet he, who was only wearing a thin shirt and an unfastened leather jacket, should feel so warm and alive?

'Let go of me,' she hissed desperately.

'I'm not touching you.'

He lifted his hands into the air to prove it, and incredibly it was true, she was actually pressing her hands against the heat of his ribs of her own volition.

She removed them as though the contact burned, snatching them away, while he laughed, a deep, unrestrained sound of male amusement.

'Why did you come to the rehearsal?' she demanded again. 'Or can I guess? It must have really amused you seeing me humiliated like that. God, you must really have enjoyed it!'

'No, I didn't.'

The flat, metallic way he said the words made her look at him. His whole face had changed. It looked harder, cruel almost, and she found herself feeling slightly afraid of the stranger she saw in him.

She hadn't feared him before, and it was an odd sensation to recognise the essential and unbreakable maleness of him, and to recognise its power. Lucilla despised most men; they were in her opinion ruled by the drive of their sex, and thereby weakened by it. Women held that ultimate power over them, but not over this man, she recognised.

He saw her fear and his expression lightened.

'I don't like seeing any fellow human being humiliated, Lucilla, especially not by someone who plainly enjoys doing it. What on earth were you doing allowing yourself to get involved with Manners in the first place? He's a first-class sadist . . .'

'I know. But bit players aren't normally consulted about who's going to direct them,' she told him with dry humour.

'Mmm . . . but casting agents are,' he told her wickedly.

'I can't work for you. What I said in there . . . I'm an actress . . .'

'No, you're *not* an actress,' he told her quietly. 'Your mother was an actress, your half-brothers are . . . but your talents lie in another direction. Give it up, Lucilla. Stop pursuing a dream that isn't yours, and accept yourself as you really are before you destroy yourself completely. Do you really want to know why I came looking for you today? When you refused to have dinner last night, I went to a party I'd been invited to. Manners was there with his boyfriend. Your name was being mentioned. You're a joke, Lucilla . . . a butt for the sadistic humour of men like him who hate you and want to humiliate you, and every time you try to act you hand them a golden opportunity to do it. Is that really what you want from life? Is it?'

'No!' She practically screamed the denial at him. 'No, it isn't . . . But I don't want to work for you, either,' she told him bitterly. She hated him for what he was doing to her, for what he was making her realise about herself . . . for the truth he kept on relentlessly pushing at her, and the last thing she wanted to do was to suffer his presence eight hours a day, listening to him telling her that she had wasted years of her life.

No one could make her work for him . . . No one could make her do anything she didn't want to do. No one ever had.

But Nick Barrington was a very special man, and as he let her walk away from him he was smiling slightly to himself. In the end he would win. He knew it.

And for his victory prize he would take that tense, unyielding, feminine body in his arms and love it until she was warm and compliant, drunk on the pleasure he was going to show her.

CHAPTER FOUR

BEATRICE greeted her with a typical flurry of anxious queries, all of which Lucilla ignored, turning her attention instead to the dark-haired, solemn little boy who was walking drunkenly toward her.

Here was one member of her family at least who had her unqualified love and approval, as she had his.

Master Dominic Elliott Chalmers' face creased into radiant smiles as he reached his goal and clung determinedly to his aunt's expensive cashmere skirt.

Lucilla prised free the small fingers and swung him into her arms.

'He's grown,' she told Beatrice.

'Hasn't he just! You wouldn't believe what a little terror he's turning into,' Beatrice told her with undisguised maternal pride. 'He's the image of Elliott, isn't he?'

'Was there ever any doubt he'd be anything else?' Lucilla asked her, watching the quick surge of colour coming and going in her half-sister's face. Why was it she could never resist the temptation to hurt Beatrice? There was a reason, but no one but she knew it, and she wouldn't have been allowed to get away with that small taunt if Elliott had been there . . . Or Benedict . . . Both men had their own ways of protecting Beatrice.

How unfair life could be; everyone adored Beatrice,

plain, dull Beatrice who didn't have an ounce of looks or talent. And yet Beatrice was loved . . . Loved in a way that she herself never would be. And Beatrice had this adorable son . . .

Lucilla frowned and checked herself. What was the matter with her? She was like Cressida, she disliked all things maternal; but unlike Cressida she was not going to hamper herself with children of her own who would hold her back and damage her career. But she wasn't like Cressida, she acknowledged uncomfortably. She actually liked the warm weight of the small body in her arms. She enjoyed the very special relationship she had with her nephew and godson.

Even Beatrice had been surprised when Elliott had nominated her as godmother for their child, along with the Italian couple who were Beatrice's friends. Had Elliott perhaps known of that odd tug of sensation she had felt that first time she had held his son; a sensation that had nothing to do with her blood relationship with Dominic, but which sprang from something deeper and far more elemental?

She had since discovered that all small children affected her in exactly the same way. She had only to hold a very young child to feel an actual physical contraction within her body; an awareness of how it had been designed to hold and nurture new life.

Whenever she stayed with Beatrice and Elliott she heard Dom cry almost before Beatrice herself did. It confused her badly, this intense awareness of her own womanliness, and so she had started paying fewer visits to her family. She suspected that Elliott knew quite well why, but Beatrice of course would suspect nothing . . . Beatrice never did.

She would be the easiest person in the world to deceive.

'You're the first to arrive. None of the others are here yet. I've put you in your usual room.'

Although Elliott had owned the house for some months before he and Beatrice were married, they had still not finished all the work they had to do on it. Apart from their own bedroom, there was only one other room with its own bathroom, and Lucilla always insisted on having it.

She had to carry her own case upstairs, because Elliott, her half-brother was out somewhere. Elliott, a highly successfully businessman, worked from home in an office above the garages which had originally been stables.

It was their intention to eventually convert the rest of the stables' upper buildings into a flat so that they could take on more staff. At present the house was run by Beatrice and Henrietta, who had once been Elliott's nanny, and whom Lucilla detested.

There were flowers in her room, two jugs full of them arranged in a pretty cottage style that looked very effective against the dark oak furniture.

Beatrice might not be glamorous or beautiful, but she was a natural homemaker, Lucilla conceded. Her bedroom smelled of fresh lavender, and there was a huge, luxurious tablet of her favourite French soap in the bathroom, plus a pile of enormous soft towels.

As a child she had resented Beatrice in a way that she had never resented Elliott. Elliott was her father's child, Beatrice was her mother's, and it had been that which she resented. Beatrice and her brothers and sister were full Bellaires, while she had only Cressida's blood.

Even so, she had been closer to Charles than any of his own children; had made a point of being so, in fact, flattering him outrageously, learning quickly how vulnerable he was to his ego and playing on that vulnerability.

It had been Charles to whom she had first confided her own ambition to act. He had paid for her to have private drama lessons. She had loved Charles in a way that she had never loved her own rather remote and shy father, and yet at the same time had resented him because he wasn't actually her father. She had felt as though he and Cressida had cheated her in some way by the fact that they had divorced, so allowing her to be born to Cressida's second husband. By right, she should have been a full Bellaire.

If she had, would it have made any difference? Would she have inherited from Charles that special something that would have made her an actress, gifted, sought after . . . a star?

'Hello, Lucilla.'

She turned back from the window at the sound of Elliott's voice. He had changed since his marriage, she reflected, studying her half-brother. He was still impossibly handsome in a hard-edged way, still as autocratic as ever, but now he was a benign autocrat, still very much in love with his wife and devoted to both her and their child.

If she and Elliott had never been particularly close, then at least they understood one another, and when he asked carelessly, 'Still dreaming impossible dreams, Lu?' she merely shrugged and smiled thinly. To her surprise, instead of dropping the subject, Elliott pressed on. 'Why don't you give it up, Lu? You're wasting your time and destroying yourself in doing so.'

'Give up what, Elliott?' she asked him bitterly. It had shaken her, to hear him speaking to her like this, so soon after she had been forced to listen to almost the same words from Nick Barrington, but she wasn't going to allow Elliott to see that.

Her half-brother possessed a razor-sharp intelligence that could be brutally probing on occasions, and she had no wish to subject herself to his scrutiny.

'This quest for stardom that you've turned into some kind of Holy Grail. There's so much more you could do with your life.'

'Settling down like you and Beatrice?' Lucilla mocked him, her face made ugly from the bitterness she couldn't prevent seeping into it. 'That's not for me, Elliott. You know that . . .'

'Neither is stardom,' he told her calmly. 'Otherwise you'd be there already.'

'I just haven't had the right breaks.' Lucilla turned away from him so that he couldn't see her face.

'Come off it. It isn't the breaks you lack, it's the talent.'

The words seemed to echo round the room, shimmering almost tangibly in the silence. This house had been built in the sixteenth century, and Lucilla wondered idly how many lives it had seen ruined and destroyed.

'Elliott.'

The sound of Beatrice's voice outside the door made Elliott frown and reach for the handle.

'Think about it, Lucilla,' he told her quietly. 'Think about what you're doing to yourself, for God's sake. Do you know what Benedict told us last weekend? That any man who wants to can take you to bed with the promise of a cheap one-line part.'

She tried not to flinch, but he saw her involuntary action and pounced on it.

'You don't like that? Well, neither do I . . .'

'And that's why you're giving me this lecture, isn't it?' Lucilla demanded. 'Because your precious pride won't allow you to have a half-sister with the reputation of being a tramp. Well, let me tell you something, Elliott. I'd sell my very soul if I thought in doing so I'd be gaining stardom.'

She said it so fiercely that for a moment Elliott said nothing.

Outside the door Beatrice called his name again. He turned the handle and said quite emotionlessly, 'Well, if that's true, Lucilla, then I'm sorry for you. You really are your mother's daughter, aren't you? Do you know, all these years I'd actually thought there was some of our father in you, that, despite all that nonsense Cressida and Charles pumped into you, you'd retain enough shrewd Chalmers hard-headedness to be able to realise that reality is far far more satisfying and enjoyable than daydreams. You'll never be a star, Lucilla. Oh, you've got the looks, you've certainly got the ego, but you haven't got any talent worth a damn, and if you haven't got the intelligence to realise it and the guts to accept it then you haven't got anything.'

He had gone before she could retaliate, letting the door swing softly closed behind him with a sound almost like a sigh.

Despite the discreetly placed radiators that provided the house with central heating, she was cold. She rubbed her arms in their covering of fine cashmere and looked out blindly over the November countryside.

Elliott was a true Scorpio, with the icy sting of death as his astral gift, and he knew exactly how to use it.

Odd, unconnected thoughts whirled through her head, small, disjointed snippets of conversation, growing and swelling until her head was filled with the mingled sound of Nick's and Elliott's voices telling her that she was a fool, destroying the frail fabric that had held together her pride and her ambition.

Of course, she knew she had no talent. No talent . . . no talent . . . the words screamed through her head over and over again, and William, opening the door to her room an hour later just ducked his head in time to avoid being hit by the very pretty Derby figurine she was hurling towards him.

'Damn you, Nick!' he heard her scream as he managed to save the figurine with a rugby tackle.

'Who's Nick?' he asked his brother-in-law conversationally later on.

'You'll have to give me another clue,' Elliott responded mildly, earning one of William's wry grins as he added, 'and at least some hint of context.'

Briefly William described what had happened,

and was surprised to see a concerned frown gather in Elliott's eyes.

'I don't know.' His frown deepened.

William had never particularly liked Lucilla, but unlike his eldest sister he wasn't frightened of her, nor, like Benedict, did he despise her. If anything, he felt mildly sorry for her, because like Elliott he was perfectly well aware of the damage his extrovert and selfishly immature parents had managed to inflict on their offspring. Only he was mercifully free of the taint of their talent and reputation, because his upbringing had been left in the hands of Beatrice, and she had a far gentler and more loving touch than their mother.

Lucilla would have benefited from some of Beatrice's tender loving care, but there were only two years between them.

Beatrice came into the room and, seeing her husband's frown, demanded worriedly, 'What's wrong?'

'I was just reminding Elliott of that first birthday party of his he invited us to,' William told her. 'Remember?'

'How could I ever forget?' Beatrice asked feelingly. 'It was to try and detach Lucilla from that dreadful TV producer. I can't remember his name . . .'

Only partially, Elliott told her promptly. 'There *was* another reason.'

William crowed with laughter when his sister blushed. 'And you didn't even realise that his birthday wasn't until November,' he teased her.

'What's really wrong?' Beatrice pressed, not in the least deceived by her husband's delicate manoeuvres.

'I'm worried about Lucilla.'

Outside the sitting-room door, Lucilla paused. The door was slightly open. Enough for her to hear Elliott's voice quite clearly, and while she hesitated Beatrice asked uncertainly, 'Why?'

'Because . . . because she's my half-sister and I love her, and because I don't want to see another Bellaire offspring being destroyed by the burden of Charles's and Cressida's reputation, although in Lucilla's case, not only was the burden willingly taken up, she's also proving stubbornly reluctant to admit it even exists, never mind to putting it down.'

'As I was too, in my own way,' Beatrice reminded him, adding quickly, 'Oh, Elliott, can't you do anything? Speak to her. When Ben started telling us about that awful gossip last week . . .'

'Yes, he did rather enjoy it, didn't he?' Elliott agreed wryly. 'But I suspect that was more because it gave him a golden opportunity to get at me than because he particularly relishes Lucilla's notoriety.'

'Do you think it's true, then?' Beatrice asked her husband uncertainly.

Outside the door Lucilla paused, wondering what kept her there, what caused that peculiar knot of tension in her stomach.

'That she's trying to buy her way to stardom with her body?' There was a pause, and then Elliott said cryptically, 'Highly unlikely . . .'

Lucilla pushed the door open, and smiled mockingly at them, noting Beatrice's flushed, guilty face, and her half-brother's calm, closed one.

'How noble of you to defend me, Elliott. So touching that you have such faith in me . . .'

'It's got nothing to do with faith. Any fool should be able to see that with your spectacular lack of stage success the very last thing you'd be any good at is playing the vamp. I don't think I've ever met a woman who dislikes and despises the male sex as much as you do, Lulu,' he added cheerfully, turning to Beatrice and ignoring her stunned expression to demand, 'Are we expecting any more of your charming siblings to join us tonight, or can we sit down and eat dinner?'

'Er—no. The twins and Miranda aren't arriving until tomorrow. Oh, and Mirry wants to bring a friend. I told her it would be all right . . .'

Lucilla heard them talking, but only the sound and not the meaning of the words reached her, like waves on a far distant shore, Elliott's throw-away, almost careless remark about her attitude toward his sex reverberating inside her skull.

She couldn't eat her dinner. Beatrice fussed over her as though she was still a child, and when Henrietta came in to remove the plates she glowered disapprovingly at Lucilla.

'Suet pastry,' Lucilla retaliated shudderingly. 'God, Beatrice, it's no wonder you're so enormous.'

In point of fact, her half-sister was a prettily rounded size twelve, and Lucilla herself only one size smaller, but because of her height she looked thinner. And not just because of her height, Lucilla acknowledged later on alone in her bedroom; these days there was a fine-drawn, brittle, nervy quality about her own looks which even in her own eyes contrasted unfavourably with Beatrice's glow of happiness and fulfilment.

Her own features were beginning to take on a sharpness, an angularity, almost as though her inner discontent were beginning to show in her face.

It was an alarming thought, and even more alarming was her own realisation that she wasn't happy. Would she ever be happy? Once she would have said that only stardom would bring her life any measure of worth, but already the dancing flames of that beckoning chimera seemed to have weakened. It was as though someone had cast a veil between her and her ultimate goal, so that somehow it seemed far off and, oddly, less appealing.

But without that lure to drive her on, what was there for her? Her whole life had been geared toward it.

There was Nick's offer of a job, a different kind of future; a future which would give full rein to her astute brain and keen organisational qualities; a future that would allow her to use to the full the contacts she had made. Where others were concerned her ability to predict their futures and her critical faculties were excellent. Even at RADA she had recognised those among her fellow students who would succeed, and she had been right.

It was also a future that offered her a much larger measure of self-respect, and that tempted her. How satisfying it would be to turn the ashes of her failure into the glowing fires of success, to see those who had scorned her viewing her with respect. To have the Julian Mannerses of this world forced to seek her advice. There were agents in Hollywood more powerful, more wealthy by far than the clients they represented; powerful, important men and women, and she could be one of them . . .

But to give up her life's ambition on the whim of one man; to turn her back on everything she had worked for?

Was that really what she wanted to do: pursue a useless dream until it destroyed her? Was she really so stubborn that she would rather destroy herself than admit the truth?

The truth? The truth was that she had little or no acting ability. How many times had she heard it over the years—heard it and ignored it? She was twenty-eight years old and this might be her last chance to turn her back on the useless folly of pursuing something she could never have and instead to reach out for something that was well within her grasp. Her own instincts told her that she could do what Nicholas asked and that she would do it well. She could see herself quite easily as the powerful, charismatic agent; the power behind the throne, so to speak. She would enjoy that power, that ability to manipulate. But to let go of so many years of her life . . . to admit she had failed . . .

'Lucilla seems different.'

Beatrice looked at her youngest sister. Mirry was beautiful, inside and out, Beatrice thought fondly, admiring the way Mirry had done her hair: all rippling curls caught back with a piece of ribbon, artless and yet fascinating at the same time . . . like Mirry herself.

Her friend had turned out to be not male, but female: a quiet, pretty girl with shy eyes and a vulnerable mouth. As she watched Benedict carelessly charming her, Beatrice felt a twinge of anger. Hadn't Benedict got the compassion to see what he might do to the poor girl? Between one smile and another she could so easily fall in love with him, and, while he would be flattered, he wouldn't care. Sometimes she wondered if the elder of the twins possessed the ability to love anyone other than himself. All the Bellaire clan were monumentally selfish, with the exception of herself, or so Elliott claimed, but in Benedict that selfishness had a dangerously egomaniacal twist that Beatrice worried about.

She switched her attention back to Mirry, frowning over her question.

'Yes. She does, doesn't she? You hear a lot of gossip, Mirry. Have you . . . ?'

'You know what the theatrical world's like,' Mirry interrupted her. 'It brings a whole new meaning to the phrase "internecine warfare". Thank God I'm not an actress. The word is that Lucilla is desperate to get the female lead in this new soap John Cassavar's launching,' Mirry told her abruptly. 'You know the one—period drama with lots of silk petticoats and swaggering buccaneers . . .' She pulled a face. 'Well, actually, there's a lot more to it than that, and the rumour is that the part Lucilla is after is going to be quite challenging, but she'll never get in, Bea . . . It's for a girl of seventeen or eighteen. If he wanted a leading lady Lucilla's age, John Cassavar would have cast his wife. She'd have been perfect for it.'

'His wife?'

'You know, Sophy Barrington. One of the Hollywood Barringtons.' She rolled her eyes and giggled. 'You must remember them! Pa never stopped mentioning them, especially when he and Ma had a fallout. You must remember how furious it used to make her. Word was that Pa had something of a fling with Helena Barrington when he was in Hollywood. Heavens, the family practically *are* Hollywood! The great-grandparents were two of the original silent movie stars, and the dynasty they started has infiltrated practically every aspect of film-making that there is. And, of course, every generation they produce at least one fabulous actor. Sophy Barrington is her generation's.'

'Oh, yes, I know who you mean now.' Beatrice wrinkled her nose. 'Are you serious about Lucilla wanting that role? I'm worried about her, Mirry. You're right, she is different. You know, Elliott thinks she might even be thinking of giving up the acting . . .'

'Before it gives her up, you mean,' Mirry commented sardonically, and then pulled a face at Beatrice's unhappy expression. 'Oh, come on, Bea! You've seen it for yourself. Lucilla is a beautiful empty shell without the slightest bit of acting ability.'

'Who are you two talking about? You both look as guilty as hell.'

Both Mirry and Beatric jumped as Sebastian strolled over to join them.

'No one who would interest you, big ears,' Mirry teased the younger of her twin brothers.

They had all arrived ten minutes earlier at the restaurant in Stratford where they were due to celebrate Elliott's birthday.

A small contretemps with the tables had resulted in

them crowding into the narrow bar to have complimentary drinks while everything was sorted out.

The restaurant Beatric had chosen was a new one, but already it had established an excellent reputation. Lucilla had heard it mentioned at a recent party she had attended, by one of the members of the company which was just coming to the end of a run of *The Taming of the Shrew*.

Once she had dreamed of being invited to join the élite company, but instead it seemed more likely that she would be acting as an agent for those who did.

Her heart gave a funny little jump then. Was it already decided, then? Had she actually relinquished her dreams of stardom, if only to her innermost self at this stage?

The head waiter was speaking to Beatrice, telling her that their table was ready, and as there was a general surge of movement into the restaurant Lucilla wondered how her family would react to the news.

Perhaps she wouldn't even tell them; at least, not until she was well established in her new way of life.

Lost in thought, Lucilla failed to see the man rising from the table adjacent to their own as she allowed herself to be carried into the room in the general swell of movement.

He excused himself to his female companion and made his way toward her. Lucilla only saw him at the last moment, stopping abruptly and awkwardly as Sebastian paused to allow him access through their massed ranks.

'Good evening, Lucilla, my lovely.'

To her shock, he bent and dropped a light kiss on

her nose.

While hardly an intimate caress, it was different enough from the usual theatrical mutual kissing of proffered cheeks for her family to pause and watch with open interest, amused by the novelty of a mere male daring to treat Lucilla like a little girl.

'Oh, Nick . . . er . . .'

Infuriatingly she was flushing, fumbling for words like a schoolgirl, while Sebastan grinned appreciatively and Benedict eyed her with speculative curiosity.

It was Beatrice who came to her rescue, saying quietly, 'Let's go and sit down. Lucilla can join us when she's ready.' But Nicholas turned round and smiled at Beatrice contritely, the smile of a man who knows he's going to be forgiven his transgressions.

'I'm sorry . . . I didn't mean to interrupt. You're celebrating Lucilla's brother's birthday, I know, and you must be Beatrice . . . I'm Nicholas Barrington. I expect Lucilla's mentioned me . . .'

Oh, how could he? How *could* he? Lucilla fumed, watching the faces of her family and seeing their varying degrees of interest and speculation.

'No . . . not a single word,' Benedict told him, extending his hand and introducing himself. 'Not like our Lulu, that . . . Normally she enjoys boasting about her latest prey.'

Lucilla could have killed him, even Beatrice frowned, but it was left to Sebastian to say calmly, 'You'll have to forgive my brother's odd sense of humour . . .'

'So you haven't told your family yet, then, Lucilla?'

He was doing it deliberately, Lucilla knew it. She

bared her teeth at him, willing him to disappear, but he didn't. He stayed right where he was, all six-foot-odd of brawn and muscle, knowing that he had the attention of all of them, and quite obviously, to her eyes at least, revelling in it.

'I came home to celebrate Elliott's birthday, Nick,' she said coldly, 'not to discuss my own private affairs . . .'

'Hardly private, darling,' Benedict drawled behind her. 'Not with the whole world and the tabloids' gossip reporters knowing all about them.'

Lucilla felt her skin burn. She ached to round on her half-brother and return his acid barb in kind, but she restrained herself, knowing already what she was going to have to endure once Nicholas dropped his bombshell.

Damn him; he was doing this deliberately, making sure there was no way she could back out of that impulsive commitment she had given to him on the spur of the moment.

'So you haven't told them yet . . . I'm sorry. I didn't mean to interfere.' His apology was accompanied by a warm smile. He was the one who should have been the actor, Lucilla thought bitterly. She was just about to turn away from him when a charming female voice with a transatlantic accent chimed in.

'Nick has just been telling us that you're going to take charge of the agency. I thought he was mad when he said he was going to buy out Max . . . Nick's an accountant, not an agent.'

'My sister, Sophy,' Nick introduced, the affection-ate warmth with which he treated his sister making

Lucilla ache a little inside, without being able to define why.

Sophy Barrington, John Cassavar's wife, and not by so much as a glance was she betraying that she knew how very different Lucilla's ambitions had been. This women *was* a star . . . It shone out of her like a radiant light; instinctively, Sebastian and Benedict were gravitating toward her, and even Mirry was staring at her in awe.

Watching the small tableau being enacted in front of them, Elliott asked quietly, 'Lucilla, is this true?'

She shrugged her shoulders tiredly.

'Why not? As you so kindly pointed out to me yesterday, I'm no actress. I've got to do something with my life, Elliott. I'm not the kind of woman who can simply settle down and raise a family. I need more from life than that.'

'What you need from life is to be able to find your own self-respect,' Elliott told her crisply, ignoring the mocking look she gave him.

Quite whose idea it was that the two parties should become one, how it came about that Nicholas started entertaining her family with reminiscences of his childhood at the British boarding-school his grandfather had decided he should attend, Lucilla didn't know, but at least his presence took off her the pressure to answer the questions she could see burning in her siblings' eyes.

She would leave for London as soon as she could in the morning. That way she could avoid answering them, although she suspected that Beatrice wouldn't let her escape easily.

She came out of her thoughts to hear her half-sister issuing a general invitation to Nicholas and his sister to join them for lunch, and on hearing her own name mentioned said quickly, 'Count me out . . . I'm catching the ten o'clock train back . . .'

'No need for that,' she heard Nicholas saying easily. 'I've got to get back early myself. I'll pick you up.'

There was absolutely nothing she could do, and she had to sit seething, mentally cursing him, and watching him giving her his narrowed, mocking tiger's smile that told her he was aware of her resentment.

CHAPTER FIVE

IN THE EVENT, it was after lunch when they eventually left. Nick arrived in plenty of time for them to leave at ten, but Benedict had overslept, having gone on to a club he knew in Stratford with Sebastian and Mirry and her friend. Lucilla, Elliot and Beatrice had declined to join them, and on discovering at nine o'clock that Benedict was still in bed, Henrietta had flatly refused to make breakfast until he was up.

Lucilla wasn't particularly hungry herself, but Dominic was vociferous in his protests at having his favourite meal of the day delayed. And so, when Nick and Sophy arrived, Mirry, who happened to be in the hallway at the time, ushered them into the kitchen without ceremony.

She grinned at the expression on Nick's face when he saw Lucilla spooning cereal into the open mouth of the child on her lap. A good deal of the sticky mixture was attached to the infant's face and hands, and there was even a smear of it on Lucilla's elegantly made-up face.

Beatrice, suddenly realising that they had guests, sprang up from her own seat, and instructed Elliott to fetch extra chairs.

The morning-room was a small, pretty room overlooking the half tamed garden, and it caught the morning sun which today was shining in, kindly highlighting the gleam on the polished oak furniture,

Beatrice's daffodil yellow curtains floating gently on the breeze through the open casement window.

'What a darling little boy! I didn't realise you had a child, Lucilla.'

Lucilla hadn't even realised that Nick and his sister had arrived, and her face burned in a mixture of shock and vulnerability at being caught at such a disadvantage.

Her eyes flashed dangerously, as though defying anyone to challenge her defences as she said quickly, 'Dominic isn't mine. He belongs to Beatrice and Elliott . . .'

'Surely you didn't really think Dominic was Lucilla's?' Benedict expostulated, insisting that Sophy sat next to him. Out of the corner of her eye Lucilla saw the expression on the face of Mirry's quiet dormouse friend. The girl looked close to tears; her hand actually trembled as she lifted her cup of coffee, and to her astonishment Lucilla found that she actually wanted to reach out and protect the girl from the knowing eyes of the rest of the family.

'She's hardly the maternal type.'

But before she could say or do anything, Nicholas, who was accepting a fresh cup of coffee from Henrietta, said quietly, 'Oh, I don't know . . .'

The effect of his words was like an electric shock running round the table. It seemed to Lucilla that everyone stopped what they were doing to look at her. She was furious with Nicholas for drawing attention to her in such a way.

She got up clumsily, passing Dominic over to Beatrice, twin spots of colour burning under her blusher.

'I think we'd better make a move,' she said tersely. 'I'll just go and get my things.'

As she turned toward the door, she paused, a sensation familiar from her childhood suddenly overwhelming her, making her feel very much an outsider.

Sophy was talking animatedly to Benedict, plainly at home in the family circle; Sebastian's head was bent close to those of Mirry and her friend, Beatrice was struggling with Dominic while Elliot turned to ask Henrietta if they could have some fresh coffee.

A feeling of loss and loneliness swept over her; a feeling that she was unimportant to all of them, an outsider to their magic circle, and then she felt Nicholas looking at her and, even though she didn't want to, she returned his regard; there was something warm and gentle in the darkness of his eyes that made her ache inside, something that she didn't want to acknowledge or respond to.

'There's no rush as far as we're concerned,' he said easily. 'Sophy's plane doesn't leave Heathrow until eight this evening.' He turned to Beatrice and explained, 'My sister is joining her husband in Hollywood. They'll be there for a few weeks, and then they're coming back here. They'll be based here then for quite some time. My brother-in-law, John, is directing and producing a new soap over here. You may have heard about it . . .'

'The period drama?' Beatrice responded. 'Yes, Mirry's been telling us about it . . .'

'It's exciting, isn't it?' Sophy asked Lucilla, breaking off her conversation with Benedict to lean across the table and address her. 'I must say, though, that I'm a bit worried about who's going to play the female lead. So much depends on her credibility, and it's going to be a very taxing role. But first Nick has to find the house. Has he told you about it yet?'

Lucilla shook her head.

'Well, as you know the series is set on an English estate in the sixteenth century, and we need to find a house of the right age and background that we can use for the series. That's what we're doing down here, actually, but so far we haven't had much luck.' She pulled a face. 'We're also going to need a base close by as well. John hates staying in hotels, and I travel with him as much as I can and when my own commitments allow. We thought we could perhaps find somewhere near to Stratford, but we need somewhere large enough to take all John's staff, as well as the girls and their nanny. We have two daughters,' she explained ruefully, 'and they're just beginning to get to the age when they hate their routine being interrupted, but we don't want them to grow up as spoiled Hollywood brats.'

'As we did,' Nick put in wryly.

Sophy pulled a face at him and said, 'What Nick really means is as I did. Nick had a much tougher time of it than me.'

'So I'm afraid you and I are going to spend a good deal of time racing up and down the motorway in the next few weeks,' Nick told Lucilla.

Before she could object or demand an explanation for his 'you and I', Beatrice broke in, exclaiming warmly, 'Oh, there's no need for that. Why don't both of you stay here and make this your base? It would make things much easier for you. We'd love to have them, wouldn't we, Elliott?' she appealed to her husband.

There was nothing Lucilla could do. Before they left for London it was all arranged. She and Nick would be spending the next two weekends with Beatrice and Elliott while they searched for a property which could be used in the series.

'I love your family,' Sophy enthused warmly once they were installed in Nick's car and speeding back to London. 'Nick and I have loads of relations—second and third cousins, that sort of thing, but no one really close. When our folks died, if it hadn't been for Grandy . . . We both have a lot to thank him for, don't we, Nick?' she appealed to her brother.

'Yes.'

The terse acknowledgement made Lucilla frown. It was so unlike Nick's normal insouciant, almost mocking manner. She looked at him in the driving mirror and saw that his eyes were dark with tension and pain.

For the rest of the journey Sophy kept them entertained with amusingly witty anecdotes about people she had met during her career.

She was the epitome of everything that Lucilla had always wanted for herself, bar the husband and the children; she was one of the most lauded actresses of her era; Lucilla knew that she ought to be both bitterly resentful and envious of her, and yet she found that she was actually drawn to her.

Lucilla had never met a woman with less vanity or

reserve; everything about Sophy was open and warm-hearted. She seemed to have no insecurities, no fears, no need to protect herself from the dangerous malice of others. When she spoke about her husband, her eyes shone with love; when she talked about her friends, it was with affection and understanding; and for the first time in her life Lucilla found herself making the first tentative and awkward steps to genuine friendship with another human being.

It was an odd experience. A healing experience, she recognised later when they had dropped her at her home, with Nick saying that he would be in touch with her in the morning.

The first thing she saw when she walked into her sitting-room was the script she had left there on Friday morning. She stared at it and then picked it up. The meaningless, trite words danced in front of her eyes, and as she tore the paper in half and then in half again with almost ritualistic concentration, she felt as though she was suddenly free of an enormous and crippling weight . . . It was the most peculiar sensation she had ever experienced—so much so that she stood completely still, concentrating all her attention on trying to analyse it.

It was several minutes before she was able to pinpoint exactly what had given rise to it. She stared at the shreds of paper in her hand, half unwilling to accept her own feelings.

It was relief, a huge and intense relief . . . that was what she was experiencing. A relief generated by the knowledge that she would never again have to study another script, never again put herself through the ordeal of auditioning, of rejection, of trying constantly striving to be a second Cressida Bellaire.

Her thoughts shifted focus, roaming at will through the past; odd memories surfacing and capturing her attention. Elliott telling her once that Beatrice was a victim of the Bellaire mystique, and that she herself was another. She had deried him bitterly at the time, but he had been right.

She had to sit down. Suddenly she felt acutely weak. The garish décor of the room hurt her eyes and she glared as it distastefully.

One of the first things she was going to do was to have to whole place redecorated.

Not in the soft, faded country cottons beloved of Beatrice, but in colours that were fresh and crisp and which reflected her own personality.

Her own personality . . . Her forehead crinkled. What was that exactly? For so long she had hidden it behind the image of her famous mother that she was no longer sure who Lucilla Chalmers actually was.

Lucilla Chalmers! Not Lucilla Bellaire, even though she had adopted her stepfather's name by deed poll. She stood up, straightening her shoulders, and walked upstairs to her bedroom.

Here, too, the décor grated, but not for much longer. She felt an extraordinary surge of energy, a need to make a completely fresh start that was intensely invigorating. She went to her bureau and found notepaper and a pen, and then sat down and started writing.

It was the coldness of her bedroom that finally made her stop, and she realised she had been working for so long that the central heating had switched itself off. She frowned at what she had written.

Long, long lists of names—fellow actors and actresses she had met over the years. She had just realised that she had an almost photographic memory for faces, and was quickly able to call to mind those which would best fit into the great Elizabethan era.

And as for the house . . . Perhaps a call to the National Trust might find what they were looking for.

She looked at the telephone. She badly wanted to ring Nick, to discuss with him her ideas and plan, but it was far too late to disturb him.

It was disconcerting how disappointed she was.

That night she had the nightmare. It had been weeks since she had last suffered it, and tonight she had not expected to be tormented by it; but she woke up just after three, awake and yet not awake, still tormented by the remembered terror, covered in sweat and yet shivering with cold. She rolled over, burying her face in her pillow, trying to suppress the tormenting memories of being alone and trapped; of intense darkness and intense cold; of the kind of panic that clawed and screamed inside her head until she was almost driven mad with it; of self-control torn into pieces and burned away as though dissolved in acid by a fear so great that nothing could subdue it.

This was the time she hated the most . . . the aftermath of the horror, when her heart pounded and her body ached, and she longed for the luxury of someone beside her to comfort her and take away the fear. But for her there would never be anyone she could trust to that extent; men might desire her, but they did not like her . . . could not love her. She was not like Beatrice. She wasn't soft and warm, but hard and dangerous, and men did not love her kind of woman.

A man's love . . . was that really what she wanted? She shivered, drawing up her knees and locking her arms round them, remembering her mother saying bitterly how much she had loved Charles, and yet he had still left her . . . still deceived her. And so she had married Elliott's father, a kind, gentle man who adored her, and she, Lucilla, was their child.

But it had been Charles whom she had loved, and after Lucilla's father's death she had gone back to him and they had remarried. Out of love . . . or out of hatred . . . ? Lucilla shivered again. All her life people had told her she was the image of Cressida, and so she had grown up believing that she must follow in her mother's footsteps. Now, suddenly, she was free of that onerous pressure, torn between discovering exactly who she really was, and clinging to the security of her familiar identity.

She fell asleep again eventually and had an odd dream. She was standing on one side of a deep chasm, a fissure in the ground, which dropped away to Stygian darkness that made her skin crawl. Behind her lay a path, along which, presumably, she had already walked, but as she looked back she saw that the path narrowed and dwindled into nothing. On the other side of the chasm, though, the path broadened out and beckoned her, but to get to it she would have to cross the chasm, and then suddenly, out of nowhere, Nick appeared on the other side of the chasm. He held out his arms to her and told her to jump, but she was too scared.

'Trust me,' he urged her. 'Trust me, Lucilla.' And she felt herself bunching her muscles ready to take the leap into the unknown, to trust that he wouldn't let her fall.

It was the sound of her own scream that woke her up; her terrified 'No!' ripping through her dream and bringing her to instant wakefulness. Her heart was pounding, her mouth dry; the dream clinging to her like an invisible net that refused to let her go.

She looked at her watch. It was half-past seven. Grimacing, she decided she might as well get up.

By half-past nine she had had her breakfast and was ready to go out. A letter, telling Julian Manners that she had resigned from the cast, was addressed and stamped.

The phone rang. She picked up the receiver.

'Lucilla, it's Nick.'

As though she hadn't already recognised his voice, sharper and more businesslike this morning, but immediately recognisable, none the less.

'I'm on my way to the office. I thought I'd stop by and pick you up.' When she said nothing, he added sharply, 'I'm not letting you back out of this, Lucilla. You've agreed to work for me, and that's exactly what you're going to do. I'll be round in ten minutes.'

He hung up before she could say a word.

A tiny thrill of excitement ran through her. She was about to embark on a completely new way of life . . . she was leaving the past behind her; and the future was a clean fresh sheet upon which only she could make any marks. This was new territory, fresh ground, untouched and virgin, and for the first time in her life she would not be trying to imitate her mother; for the first time in her life she would be judged as Lucilla Chalmers, not as Cressida Bellaire's daughter.

She heard Nick rap on the front door and went to open it. He looked surprised to find her dressed and ready to leave, but he eyed the letter she was carrying with a frown, and demanded abruptly, 'What's that?'

'My resignation.'

She saw his expression change and grow bitter.

'Damn you, Lucilla, I've already told you. I'm not letting you back out of this. Together you and I are going to make this agency the best in London.'

It gave her an odd thrill of emotion to realise that he was angry because he thought she had changed her mind.

'That's right,' she agreed blandly, giving him a triumphant little smile. 'But first I have to tell Julian that I'm quitting the play. That's what this is.'

He actually seemed to lose colour, the bones in his face sharply delineated beneath the taut skin. It amazed her that such a very powerful and strong man could show such vulnerability. Was it really so important to him?

'Why are you so determined to have me working for you?' she asked him as he helped her into her car.

He waited until he was seated beside her, with the engine started, before answering. As he pulled out into the busy traffic, he glanced at her and said briefly, 'I need your expertise. I'm not familiar with the acting scene over here. But you are . . . no one more so. You know everyone there is to know in this business, Lucilla. You come from a family like my own, and when I first heard about you I guessed that you could be useful to me. When I met you I knew it.'

He didn't say any more, concentrating instead on his driving. What he had said was quite true, and yet at the same time it was oddly deflating. What was the matter with her? Lucilla derided herself. At long last she had met a man who wanted her for something other than her body, and she was feeling peeved because he hadn't made any physical overtures toward her!

Max's offices were in a prestigious block that provided some precious car parking spaces, and Lucilla was surprised to discover that Nick had designated one of these as hers.

She was even more surprised when he ushered her up to the offices themselves and she discovered that she had her own room with her name already on the door.

'What if I hadn't agreed to take the job?' she asked him derisively,

'Sometimes it's worth while taking things on trust—having a little faith,' he replied.

His answer surprised her, but not as much as the bleak look that hardened his mouth. It was the look of a man who'd known what it was to have his trust abused. By whom? she wondered. It must have been a woman, it always was . . . but which woman? She was surprised to discovered how much she resented her. Surprised and dismayed, but there wasn't time to go too deeply into her feelings, for Nick was talking about the role he envisaged her playing in the agency.

'For the next few months we'll be pulling out all the stops. John wants me to co-ordinate things for his new soap, and I'll be calling on your help there, and then there's the day-to-day business of the agency as well. You'll be completely in charge of that.

'We're bound to lose clients at first,' he warned her, 'so don't be too down-hearted when it happens. By the time *Queen's Caprice* hits the TV screens, I can almost guarantee that we'll get back far more than we've lost.'

He had a shrewd business mind, acute and sharp, Lucilla recognised, sensing how much he enjoyed the cut and thrust of the way he earned his living.

Over the next few days she discovered how extensive his business interests actually were. Nicholas Barrington was an extremely wealthy and successful man, with interests that ranged far outside the world of Hollywood and all that it embraced.

In fact, the agency was no more than a small side-line, and, from something Sophy had let drop during a transatlantic phone call, she guessed that Nick had taken on the co-ordination of everything necessary to begin filming on *Queen's Caprice* more as a favour to his brother-in-law than as a business enterprise.

Certainly he intended devoting a good deal of their mutual time to it. Work at the agency was put on 'hold' for at least a fortnight while she and Nick looked for both suitable accommodation for his sister and her family, and a house they could use for filming purposes.

Nick had liked her suggestion of approaching the National Trust about the latter, and Beatrice rang up on Thursday to say that she had canvassed all their local estate agents about the former.

'I've got tons of stuff for you to go through here,' she told Lucilla enthusiastically. 'What time will you arrive tomorrow? Henry wants to know what she should do about meals.'

Lucilla placed her hand over the receiver and looked at Nick, who was talking to Charlotte at the other end of the office. A cool wariness existed between lucilla and the secretary, neither of them fully prepared to trust the other as yet. She called over to Nick and he came toward her.

'It's Bea . . . She wants to know what time we'll be arriving tomorrow.'

'I'll have a word with her.'

He had to reach across her to take the receiver, and she was curiously conscious of the warmth of his body and its male scent. She stood frozen within the arch of his arm, her skin prickling with a sensation that was totally unfamiliar. One part of her yearned to move closer to him, the other was terrified by the unexpectedness of that yearning and froze her to the spot where she stood. If she turned her head she would be within inches of touching him, able to warm the brown skin of his throat with her breath and to feel his on her forehead. Instead she fixed her attention on the receiver, watching as his hand caught hold of it.

He had long, lean fingers, hard and slightly calloused in places, as though at one time he had worked outside. His skin was brown, his wrists sinewy and male, shadowed with the dark hair that disappeared into the cuff of his shirt.

An impossible sensation gathered in the pit of her

stomach, causing her whole world to shift focus; she tried to breathe and discovered that she couldn't; her throat was seized in terrified paralysis, her heart thumping with terror. She looked at his nails, trying desperately to focus on something and regain her self-control. They were clean and well shaped. She drew a shaky breath, feeling the tension ease out of her and unlock her muscles.

'Yes, we'll be there in plenty of time for dinner. I thought we'd have a leisurely drive down. Have lunch somewhere . . .' She heard him laugh. 'Oh, she deserves it. She's worked hard this week.' She saw his free hand replace the receiver and stared mutely at it, still shaken by the intensity of what she had just experienced.

'Lucilla . . .'

She focused on him, her mouth soft and slightly tremulous, her eyes blind with shock and disbelief.

'Lucilla,' he said her name again, more gently, and reached out to touch her shoulder.

At his touch Lucilla became instantly aware of what was happening to her and where she was. He was man . . . the enemy; she tensed and flashed him a bitter look, stepping back from him.

'I've told Beatrice we'll be down in time for dinner,' he told her equably, ignoring her abrupt withdrawal. 'Will that suit you?'

'Yes . . .'

'No Friday-night date?'

'I don't date.'

The moment the betraying words were out, she tensed warily, but he appeared not to notice the vehemence of her statement, turning his attention back to the document he had been studying when the telephone rang.

'There are John's suggestions for the lead female role.' He passed her a list of actresses' names. 'Have a look at them and tell me what you think.'

'You already know what I think,' Lucilla told him, refusing to take the printed sheets.

'Tracy Hammond. Yes, I know. But she's heavily involved in filming at the moment.'

'Only for the next few months. John's filming schedule could be revised, and the shots that don't need her done first.'

'You're really that convinced?'

Lucilla nodded, and then demanded aggressively, 'That's what you hired me for, wasn't it? My ability to find the right person for the right role . . .'

'Look, I'm not arguing with you . . . As a matter of fact, I agree. She would be ideal for the part. She has that glowing, fey quality about her, combined with an intelligence that would be exactly right for the period. The kind of woman we're talking about is no pretty bimbo with nothing between her ears other than cotton wool. She's a shrewd, clever woman, who has to run her husband's estate in his absence, and keep their enemies at bay.'

'And to keep the Queen's goodwill,' Lucilla reminded him. 'And that couldn't have been easy. Elizabeth wasn't overly fond of her own sex.'

'I'll have a word with John and see what he thinks, but he won't be keen on changing his schedule,' he warned her.

Lucilla shrugged her shoulders and said sweetly, 'Then it will be your job to make him keen, won't it? I've already done mine. You asked for my suggestions and you've got them.'

'I have, indeed,' he agreed, looking at the extremely comprehensive list of names she had given him during her first day at the office. Alongside each name was a detailed list of their careers, and a brief but authoritative comment on why Lucilla thought they would be good for each specific role.

'I see you've mentioned your half-brothers here.'

'Not out of nepotism,' Lucilla assured him drily. 'In fact, I can't stand Ben and the feeling is mutual, but they are both of them well-established actors, and if they can be released from their stage contracts and they're willing to play the parts, you won't be able to get anyone better.'

'And of course having twins to play the role of twins will make filming a lot easier,' Nick agreed. 'I see you've put Sebastian down for Kit.'

Kit was the more extrovert and daring of the twin sons of a local landowner, who in the story changed places with the other so that Kit could woo the heroine in her husband's absence.

'I thought he was the quieter of the two.'

'He is,' Lucilla agreed, 'but he'll be much better than Ben at conveying the emotional impact of Kit's discovery that he is actually in love with Tabitha.'

Nick was looking at her in a way that made her ask defensively, 'What's wrong?'

'Nothing,' he told her drily. 'I was just marvelling at your complete lack of ability to recognise your own talent, when you show such a remarkable degree of astuteness in seeing it in others . . .'

He saw the look of doubt and defensiveness cross her face and added softly, 'I'm paying you a compliment, Lucilla.'

And so he had. But it wasn't until much later, when she was alone, that she was able to examine the words and gloat over them. For the first time in her life she had received recognition of a talent that was entirely her own. For the first time in her life she felt confident, both in herself and in her ability.

It had been startling to discover how much she enjoyed working at the agency, how satisfied she felt when she was able to slot the right person into the right role. Sending someone for an audition and then discovering that they had got the part gave her an enormous sense of satisfaction that had nothing to do with power or any pleasure in manipulating people to suit her own designs, but sprang entirely from knowing that her judgement had been accurate, and the hitherto unfamiliar sensation of a job well done.

It was a completely new way of life, and it seemed to bring forth new aspects of her personality. The acid bitterness with which she had treated other people and which had sprung from her own deep-seated insecurities began to give way to a crisp professionalism that demanded and got the respect of those with whom she was dealing.

In the evening when she got home, her head was spinning with facts and thoughts, with things done and to be done, but the tension which in the past had gripped her spine like a metal fist, causing her sleepless nights and severe headaches, was gone.

She even looked better, she acknowledged in some surprise, which was odd because she now had far less time to spend worrying about her make-up and appearance.

She found she had a new energy and resoluteness, a determination to succeed which had nothing to do with her old relentless striving for stardom.

And the catalyst that had caused the transformation was Nick. Nick, whom she sometimes surprised looking at her with watchful, guarded eyes; Nick, who teased her and mocked her, and yet who never once showed the slightest degree of sexual interest in her.

That niggled her slightly, like someone touching a tender spot. Never once in the past had any of the men she had vamped into giving her jobs and then dropped without fulfilling the promises implicit in her determined come-ons ever had the slightest doubts that she was what she pretended to be; not one of them had ever challenged her sexuality, or suspected the truth. So why should Nick?

Just because he wasn't interested in her sexually? That didn't mean he was aware of her inhibitions and fears. Why should he be? No one else was.

She ought to have been reassured by his calm, almost fraternal manner toward her, but she wasn't.

And that worried her.

CHAPTER SIX

'THIS is an almost idyllic spot.'

They were parked on the roadside on the crest of a hill that gave them a view of Beatrice and Elliott's home and the surrounding countryside.

'They get snowed in in winter,' Lucilla responded drily.

'You don't like the country?'

Nick restarted the car, and looked over his shoulder at the oncoming traffic.

'I don't dislike it,' Lucilla told him judiciously. It was true. She had no strong feelings one way or the other. Since leaving RADA, her life had been centred in London. She enjoyed the amenities of living in a capital city, but she wasn't immune to the pleasure of walking on an early spring or crisp autumn day. She didn't like the cold, and normally took her summer holidays somewhere hot like Greece.

'What about you?'

'I like it,' Nick told her. 'I was at boarding-school over here, and now I find I miss it when I'm back in the States.'

He had mentioned attending a British boarding-school before. It wasn't uncommon, but she wondered what caused the tightening of his face when he mentioned his schooldays.

'Was Sophy over here at school as well?' she asked

curiously.

He shook his head, his 'No,' curt, warning her not to press the subject.

'Have you got that list the National Trust gave us?' he asked her.

'Yes. I've arranged for us to visit the most promising ones this weekend. Most of them are fairly local, although it could be difficult arranging a filming schedule. Most of them are open to the public a good deal of the time,' she warned him.

In fact, none of the houses listed by the National Trust had really been what they were looking for. Most of them were too grand, with so much later architecture added that it would be difficult to use them and maintain the Elizabethan ambiance of the series.

They were well into November, and the light was fading from the afternoon sky as they drove down toward their destination.

It had been raining earlier in the day, and now the sky was pale grey and lemon where the weak sun had finally emerged from the clouds.

They had to drive through the village, its shops and cottages warmly lit, its one street busy with the bustle of a Friday afternoon.

Nick stopped to allow a woman with two children to use the pedestrian crossing. The children were dressed in bright green ski suits with red and blue appliquéd ducks across the front. One of them dropped a red mitten, and Nick waited patiently for her to pick it up.

The child's hood slipped back, revealing a mass of soft blonde curls.

'I suppose you must have looked like that.'

Lucilla stared at him.

'Did you have a happy childhood, Lucilla?' he asked her abruptly.

She answered him equally shortly. 'No. I was bitterly jealous of Beatrice, and I hated the fact that my mother was always away. We had a nanny. I loathed her. She . . .'

She broke off, surprised that she had told him so much. She hated discussing her childhood, and very rarely did.

'Did you?' she questioned him.

He nodded. 'Yes, but for a while my memories of it were tainted by the miseries of my early adolescence. I think your sister's children are going to be very fortunate.'

'Because Beatrice is the dedicated wife and mother type?'

'No. Because both their parents know the dangers of exposing children to the egos of insecure adults. Is this the turning?'

It was, and she was left to consider his comment in silence as he drove down the drive.

Beatrice was at the front door to welcome them inside.

'I saw your lights,' she explained, and then laughed as Dominic came rushing into the hall with a one-year-old's unsteady gait, and launched himself at Lucilla, clutching her around her knees and chanting his private and unintelligible version of her name.

He made a noisy protest when Beatrice tried to lift

him away, and so Lucilla bent down and picked him up instead. He beamed at her, tangling sticky fingers in her hair.

Behind her, she heard Beatrice explaining softly, 'He adores Lucilla; when she's here I can't keep him away from her.'

'Yes, odd, isn't it? The child obviously has no taste.'

Lucilla's heart sank as Ben strolled into the hall, watching her with malicious and amused eyes.

'Poor darling. Not quite your usual style of accessory.'

'Ben,' Beatrice admonished him sharply.

'I'll take you straight up to your rooms,' she told Lucilla and Nick. 'We're having dinner about eight. Elliott had to go out, but he should be back soon. Oh, and I think I might possibly have found you a house . . . I was having lunch witht he vicar's wife the other day, and she happened to mention that the owner of Arlington Manor has had to go to the States on business for six months, and that he's looking for a tenant. I don't think you were with us when we went around it, Lucilla. It's about ten miles from here. A lovely place—not large, but Tudor and with the most beautiful garden. Anyway, to cut a long story short, I've arranged that you can see the house if you think it might be of interest. A local estate agent is responsible for letting it, and he's quite happy for you to have the keys. In fact, I've got them here.'

'Well, it certainly sounds worth while investigating, doesn't it, Lucilla?' Nick responded.

Lucilla waited for the familiar surge of resentment; the anger and bitterness she always felt when someone upstaged her, however innocently, but instead she was far too excited at the prospect of seeing the house, which from Beatrice's description sounded as though it might be ideal.

'It does,' she agreed, 'and since Bea's got the keys, we could check it before we go and inspect the others.'

She heard Beatrice expel her breath, and realised that her half-sister was looking relieved.

'I was dreadfully worried that you might think I was interfering, but the house is so beautiful . . .'

'Not at all. We're glad of all the help we can get, aren't we, Lucilla?' Nick responded easily.

'Yes,' she agreed, adding drily, 'especially in finding something for Sophy. It must have at least six bedrooms, all with their own private bathrooms, a study, a drawing-room, a dining-room, a swimming pool . . .'

'The simple, basic things in life, they're what appeal to my sister,' Nick said with a grin. 'I've tried to tell her that England isn't Hollywood, but I don't think I've got through to her yet.'

'Well, she did say they could manage with three bathrooms,' Lucilla pointed out to him, 'and when I spoke to her on the phone yesterday, she said we could forget about the swimming pool.'

'Magnanimous of her,' Nick said drily.

'Will you stay with them while they're filming?' Beatrice asked him.

Nick shook his head.

'No, I shan't be involved in that side of things. Lucilla and I will be back at our desks, deftly slotting square pegs into square holes, shan't we?'

'But you've got a lot of money tied up in this production.'

Lucilla stared at Ben, her forehead creasing. How had her half-brother known that? She certainly hadn't. She had guessed from the odd comment he had made that Nick wasn't a poor man, but she had had no idea he was wealthy enough to invest in something as big as a major TV series.

'As an investor,' Nick agreed coolly, 'but that's as far as my interest goes. I'm an accountant, not a director or a producer. I prefer to leave that side of things to the experts.'

Lucilla had the feeling that Nick didn't altogether like Benedict, and that cheered her up.

She was so used to people praising her half-brother for his looks and talent that she had begun to feel that she must be the only person who found him malicious and unkind.

Not, of course, that his antagonism was entirely undeserved. There had been many times in the past when they had been bitter enemies, and of the two she had always preferred Sebastian, with his kinder, less abrasive personality.

Dom was beginning to feel heavy, and she shifted him to her other hip, grimacing as he tugged protestingly at her hair.

Beatrice was walking toward the stairs, with Nick at her side. Lucilla fell into step behind them, and was startled when Ben came alongside her and murmured tauntingly, 'Are you trying to impress him with your feminine skills, darling? I must say I applaud your good sense. You aren't getting any younger, are you? And a rich husband can always be considered a good asset, providing you can get him to the altar. Rumour has it that he's very choosy. A couple of semi-serious relationships, and none of the bed-hopping one might expect. Perhaps he's learned by his mother's mistakes. Odd that he doesn't look the least like his sister.'

Lucilla paused to remove Dom's finger from her ear and said irately, 'Oh, for heaven's sake, Ben, what on earth are you talking about?'

'The fact that Nicholas Barrington may not be a Barrington at all.'

Out of the corner of her eye, Lucilla saw Nick hesitate between one step and the next, and wondered if he had overheard Ben's acid comment.

'I wonder what it is he wants from you, Lucilla?'

'Why should he want anything?' she said carefully, but her heart was beginning to thump uncomfortably, and, although she told herself it was carrying Dom's weight that was causing it, she knew it wasn't true. How many times recently had she asked herself the same question?

'Well, whatever it is, it certainly isn't sex,' Ben told her mockingly. 'I've seen him looking at Bea with more interest than he's shown you.'

'Just because he isn't constantly pawing me in public, it doesn't mean that he doesn't want me,' Lucilla flashed back instantly.

Ben had unerringly found where she was most

vulnerable, and she retaliated instantly and defensively, like anyone under attack.

'So you *are* lovers.' Ben looked amused. 'Well, well, I thought he had better taste.'

They were almost at the top of the stairs. Beatrice and Nick were waiting for them. Lucilla forced a tight smile; her face felt as though the muscles had been set in concrete. She felt sick inside, sick and in despair. Why on earth had she allowed Ben to trap her into that silly lie? He was bound to discover the truth. He only needed to question Nick . . .

It shouldn't have mattered that he would find out that she had lied, but it did. From childhood, Lucilla had been conscious of Ben's desire to pull her down, to make her look small. There had always been a sharp rivalry between them, and she knew how much he would enjoy finding her out. He would crow over it, repeating the story in front of his friends, humiliating her. And there wasn't a thing she could do about it.

'Lucilla, are you all right? You've gone quite pale,' Bea asked anxiously.

'It's your son. He's heavy,' she fibbed, disengaging the small bundle and handing him back to Beatrice. Her arms felt empty without him, and she was tempted to reach out and take him back.

'Dinner at eight,' Beatrice reminded them outside their respective doors. She had put them in adjoining rooms. Did *she* think they were lovers? Lucilla gnawed at her bottom lip and frowned. Perhaps she'd be lucky and get away with it. Perhaps Ben wouldn't realise . . .

There were only five of them for dinner, but what should have been a relaxed family meal turned out to be a nightmare for Lucilla, who lived in dread of Ben making some comment about her and Nick being lovers.

It struck her, as she tried to look as though she was enjoying Henry's meal, that this was the first time she had ever worried about how a man might react on discovering that he was supposed to be her lover. In the past she had simply assumed that no man could resist the boost to his ego, and it had certainly never occurred to her to be concerned that he would know that she had been lying about their relationship.

But Nick was different. *She* was different. She tensed, her hand arrested in the act of carrying a forkful of food to her mouth.

'Lucilla, what's wrong?'

She looked blankly at Beatrice, and then realised that everyone was staring at her.

For once her normal aplomb deserted her. She knew that they were all waiting for her to say something that would explain away her sudden tension, but she could think of nothing.

In the end, it was Nick who came to her rescue saying humorously, 'I expect Lucilla is plotting on how best she can convince Tracy Hammond that she has to take the part of Tabitha—the female lead in John's new soap,' he added by way of explanation. 'Lucilla is convinced that Tracy would be perfect for the part, and I'm inclined to agree with her. She'll make an ideal Tabitha.'

'Hear that, Lucilla?' Ben commented goadingly. 'It looks like Nick has found his ideal woman.'

Across the table Lucilla glared at him, knowing quite well what he was trying to do, but before she could say anything Nick himself interrupted calmly. 'Not in Tracy. An ideal *actress* for the part of Tabitha, yes, but an ideal woman . . . First one would need to be an ideal man.'

Elliott and Beatrice laughed, and Beatrice asked curiously, 'If I'm not prying, what would constitute your "ideal woman", Nick? I must confess I'm always fascinated to see how very differently the male sex views these things from the female.'

'Well, let me see . . .'

Although Lucilla herself wasn't conscious of it, Bea noticed the quick glance he gave her half-sister before he started to speak. Lucilla looked tense and on edge.

She was. The very last thing she wanted to do was to hear Nick raving over some fictional ideal of feminine perfection, or worse still drawing a verbal portrait that was all too easily recognisable. Not after what she'd told Benedict. She hadn't missed the easy, teasing camaraderie which had quickly developed between Nick and Bea, and she was resentful of it. Stupidly so, she told herself.

'She'd be beautiful, of course, with the kind of beauty that comes from inside rather than out; intelligent, warm, independent enough for me to always feel that life with her was a challenge, and yet at the same time so much in love with me that she'd gladly abandon her high-powered career to be at my side.'

This was said with tongue in cheek, making Elliott and Bea laugh again, and Bea exclaimed, 'An ideal, indeed. Have you found her yet?'

It was a light-hearted question, but Nick's face changed, and Lucilla felt the oddest sensation grip her body as he looked right into Bea's eyes and said quietly, 'I think so, but it isn't going to be easy convincing her.'

Nick was practically making verbal love to Bea under Elliott's nose, and to Lucilla's rage and astonishment her half-brother did nothing at all about it.

Indeed, the three of them, Nick, Bea and Elliott, seemed to be linked together in a silent communication which excluded Lucilla and Benedict completely.

'Take care, Nick,' Benedict said lightly, obviously coming to the same conclusion as Lucilla. 'Elliott is a very jealous husband . . .'

Unlike her, Elliott did not respond to Benedict's goading, Lucilla noticed. In fact he seemed to be remarkably unmoved by what had just happened, and Bea, far from looking uncomfortable or embarrassed, was smiling very happily.

Elliott was saying something to Nick, and under cover of their conversation Benedict murmured dulcetly to her.

'Well, well, Lucilla, looks like your lover's turning his attention in another direction already. Remarkable how short-lived these affairs of yours can be.'

She couldn't be bothered to retaliate. She was too numbed by the discovery of how she felt about the possibility of Nick desiring Bea.

There had been far more than mere gallantry in that long look they had exchanged, as though the two of them shared a very private knowledge, and yet no one could describe Bea as independent, much less high-powered. Bea was no career woman . . .

What was she trying to do—convince herself that Nick couldn't possibly be attracted to Bea, when she had seen with her own eyes that he was?

What had she wanted—to hear him describe *her* as his ideal woman? Some chance! It was a shock to feel the sharp stab of pain that followed that acknowledgement.

She realised that Elliott and Nick had stopped talking and that Nick was turning toward her. The last thing she wanted right now was to talk to him. She felt too on edge, too stunned by the realisation of how hurt she had been by his praise of Bea, and she was relieved when Beatrice announced, 'Henry's going out tonight. I'd better start clearing the table,' starting up, as she did so.

'I'll give you a hand,' Lucilla said quickly, refusing to look at Nick.

It was hardly surprising that her half-sister looked stunned, Lucilla admitted, recalling her normal practice of simply sitting back and allowing others to wait on her.

Henrietta had been Elliott's nanny when he was a little boy, and she had been with Beatrice and Elliott ever since they had married. She adored them both, although she would have died rather than admit it, and she frowned admonishingly now as Bea and Lucilla walked into the kitchen with the empty plates.

'Don't you go dropping those, Lucilla.' She whisked the plates away before Lucilla could protest. Behind her back Bea grimaced sympathetically, and admitted wryly once they were out of earshot, 'I'm sure she doesn't think I'm capable of looking after either Elliott or Dom properly, you know.'

Lucilla, who had always resented Beatrice's domestic efficiency, looked at her in surprise and Beatrice chuckled.

'I'm sorry Ben was such a pig at dinner,' she apologised soberly. 'I don't know what gets into him at times.'

'It wasn't your fault,' Lucilla told her drily. Ben had always been Bea's champion, but he was also extremely possessive where his elder sister was concerned. Lucilla suspected that he saw Bea as a substitute mother figure, and she knew he had bitterly resented her marriage to Elliott.

'I'm glad you're so happy in your new job, Lucilla,' Bea told her impulsively. 'Elliott's been concerned . . .'

She broke off and looked uncomfortable, and Lucilla supplied wryly for her, 'That I'd never admit that I was wasting my time trying to be an actress. I think I knew it a long time ago, but I grew up believing that nothing was as important as being a successful actress.'

'You and me both,' Beatrice said ruefully.

They exchanged a long look of mutual understanding; the first tentative sensation of genuine awareness of her half-sister as a potential friend and not a resented rival stirred inside Lucilla.

'There are other and far more worth while things in life, though,' Beatrice said softly. 'It's almost like a family curse, isn't it—this intense need to follow in our parents' footsteps? Although I think William has escaped it, and Mirry to some extent, too.'

A family curse. That was one way of putting it, Lucilla mused thoughtfully as she and Beatrice went to join the men in the drawing-room.

An odd silence greeted them. Ben was looking as smug as a cat full of cream, and a tiny rustle of apprehension slid down Lucilla's spine.

Instinctively she looked at Nick, but he was studying his fingernails intently.

Elliott made some comment about the proximity of Christmas, and Beatrice agreed with him, asking Lucilla if there was any chance that she would be able to join them. Normally she spent Christmas in Switzerland with friends: a noisy, impersonal party who all made a point of mocking the dull and boring traditions of family Christmases. For some reason, this year the idea palled, but before she could say anything Ben purred, 'But surely you'll be spending it with Nick . . .'

Beatrice looked puzzled.

'Oh, are you so busy, then?' she asked. 'I hadn't realised.'

Ben said wickedly, 'Oh, how naïve of you, my darling sister, and after having known Lucilla all her life as well. Nick is Lucilla's latest lover.'

There was an uncomfortable pause and Beatrice flushed.

'You know, Ben,' Elliott remarked urbanely, 'there are times, increasing in number of late, when I find that you remind me of the most obnoxious kind of grubby little schoolboy.' But it was too late, the damage was done, and Lucilla couldn't wait to escape to her bedroom so that she could be alone.

In the event she was delayed from getting there by Beatrice who wanted to give her the keys and directions on how to find the manor house.

'I'm sorry about Ben,' she apologised in a low tone. 'He was unbearable tonight. He's always been unbearable to you because you were so close to Mum and Dad. I think he always resents the fact that you were their favourite.'

Their favourite. Yes. She had been, but at what a price! She had totally sublimated her own ego as a teenager, in order that she could pander to theirs, had slavishly worshipped everything they said and did, and at the same time had quite blatantly played upon Charles's vanity so that he saw his sons as rivals and resented them for it, and all because she had so desperately craved their love. But had she had it? Had any of them? Had either of the Bellaire parents been capable of loving anyone other than themselves? It was a chilling thought.

She said goodnight to Beatrice and walked upstairs to her bedroom, opening the door still deep in thought.

Nick was sitting on her bed.

'Close the door,' he instructed her icily.

She did so, staring at him, her eyes luminous, her mouth vulnerable.

'Would you care to explain to me how Ben comes to have the idea that you and I are lovers?'

She wanted to tremble, but she suppressed the weakness. Nick had every reason to be angry; she had been prepared for him to be, but she hadn't been prepared for this icy contempt, this stranger who suddenly seemed to be inhabiting the body of the easy-going man she thought she knew.

'I told him we were. He was goading me . . . taunting me.'

'Taunting you?'

Lucilla checked herself. How could she tell him the truth? That it was her own vulnerability and inner fear that someone would discover the truth that had motivated her.

Shrugging, she arched her eyebrows and asked carelessly, 'Is it really so important? Ben assumed we were lovers. I could see that nothing I was going to say would change his mind.'

'Didn't it occur to you that I might not be too happy about his assumptions?'

It was even worse than she had expected. She had known he would be angry, but she had not known how much his anger would hurt.

'Of course,' he said sarcastically. 'I'm forgetting. I'm supposed to be flattered at the prospect, aren't I? Times are changing, Lucilla,' he told her cruelly, 'and I don't find it in the least flattering to be linked sexually with a woman who's reputed to have been to bed with every man who's ever offered her a job, as well as a good many who haven't.

'Real women don't need to prove their sexuality so publicly, but then you aren't real, are you, Lucilla? You're just a beautiful face and a cold, calculating little heart. Well, I'm not going to play your game with you. The next time you tell anyone that you and I are lovers, you'd better be able to back that claim, and we both know that will never be the case. You're the last woman I'd want to take to bed.'

Even if she'd wanted to defend herself, she couldn't have done. She was incapable of saying a single word. She watched him stride to the door without looking at her. He closed it behind him and she stared at the polished oak without really seeing it.

With less than a hundred savage words he had ripped apart her defences, and left her torn and bleeding.

It didn't matter that he'd confirmed what she had already known, that sexually he didn't find her desirable; it didn't even matter that he was furious with her for lying to Ben; what did matter was that she had thought he was her friend, that she had thought, idiotically, that he had seen through the image she presented to the outside world, and even though he had not known what they were, had known of her vulnerabilities. She had thought he had known that she would never treat him the way she had treated other members of his sex.

She undressed and showered mechanically,

hoping against hope that he would come back and say it was all a mistake, but he didn't.

She curled up in the huge king-sized bed feeling more lonely than she had ever felt in her life.

CHAPTER SEVEN

IN THE MORNING, Lucilla half expected to find that Nick had left during the night, but no, he was there in the kitchen, talking to Henrietta and drinking coffee. The 'good morning' he gave her was cool and businesslike.

Henrietta frowned over her refusal of breakfast and commented forthrightly, 'Well, you should. You're too thin, and if you're not careful, young lady, you'll end up looking scraggy.'

Lucilla ignored her, pouring herself a cup of coffee and drinking it in numb silence.

'We'll leave whenever you're ready,' Nick told her curtly. 'The manor house first, I think, and then the National Trust places.'

Lucilla had already planned out a route during the week, and it was tucked away inside the leather shoulder-bag along with notepad, dictaphone, pens and a comprehensive map.

Henrietta offered to make them sandwiches, but Nick refused.

'It's a cold day. We'll probably want to stop and have something for lunch.'

Henrietta compromised by giving them a flask of hot coffee and some home-made scones.

They walked out to Nick's car in silence. When he got to the bottom of the drive, Lucilla gave him instructions in a clipped, cold voice. She was petrified of betraying to him how much their quarrel had upset her.

As he watched the traffic, she snatched a quick look at his profile. It was set and hard.

A terrible sense of bleakness gripped her and she shivered, remembering how as a child she had often been conscious of her mother's total indifference to her. She had suffered then, and she was suffering now. But Nick wasn't her mother; she couldn't court his attention with flattery.

'Which way now?' he demanded tersely, and she realised they had come to a crossroads.

She fumbled with the directions and dropped them. Nick cursed and stopped the car, and as she scrabbled on the floor for them he reached down for them, too.

The warmth of his body so close to her own, combined with his mental and emotional distance, heightened her sense of isolation and loss. Suddenly she felt she had to tell him the truth, to explain to him why she had let Ben think they were lovers. Even though it would reveal to him all her vulnerabilities, at least he would know that she hadn't lied out of vanity.

'Nick, about last night, I wanted to tell you . . .'

'Don't tell me anything. I don't want to hear any more lies,' he silenced her harshly. 'I thought I'd actually got through to the woman behind the empty mask, but I was deceiving myself, wasn't I, Lucilla? That mask is all there is . . . There is no real woman.'

Lucilla couldn't say a word. She could only sit there and use every ounce of self-control she had left to stop herself from crying.

As it was, she saw the manor house through a blur of tears that made it seem to shimmer slightly, as though it were more mirage than real.

As Bea had said, it wasn't large, but it was of beautifully mellow Cotswold stone that didn't even lose its golden glow in the darkness of the overcast November day.

A rutted lane led to the house past the walled garden and into a cobbled yard surrounded by the bulk of the house itself and its outbuildings. There was a well in the centre of the courtyard with an old-fashioned iron pump, and as Lucilla opened the car door she could hear the cooing of doves.

She knew even before she set foot inside that the house would be perfect, and it was, right down to the clipped yews that bordered some of the paths.

A maze of small rooms and passages led to the front of the house and its main reception rooms: a panelled library, a formal drawing-room, a small sitting-room and another panelled room that was obviously used as a dining-room.

The scent of roses and beeswax hung elusively on the air, and Lucilla could have sworn that if she closed her eyes she would be able to visualise Tabitha walking into the room and raising the jewelled, scented pomander to her nose to inhale the rich perfume of cloves and musk as she asked them what she wanted.

'It's perfect.'

They were the first words either of them had said, and they seemed to hang on the silence.

'Yes,' Nick agreed. 'But we'd better check upstairs.'

One of the requirements of the script was that the house they used must have a long gallery; very fashionable in Elizabethan times as a means of exercise and entertainment in inclement weather.

The stairs were narrow and ancient, but the gallery was there, complete with discreetly secluded window-seats and shadowy corners.

'You take this end. I'll do the other,' Nick suggested crisply, leaving her to walk the length of the gallery.

Lucilla opened the door to the first bedroom. It was panelled like the library downstairs, with a large casement window that overlooked the front gardens.

The four-poster bed, although surely not original, was heavy enough to look authentic. This could be Tabitha's room, once she was mistress of the house.

They could probably film her sitting in the window, watching the approaches to the house. Lucilla tried it to see if it would be feasible.

The leaded lights obscured the view slightly, and she leaned back against the panelling, trying to get a better view. There was a soft click and then she was falling into thick, black, smothering darkness. She screamed out, the sound silenced as she landed on something cold and hard, the impact knocking her breath from her lungs, as she caught the side of her head on something cold and hard. For a moment she felt sick and dizzy, but she subdued the feeling.

Apart from being winded, she didn't appear to have hurt herself.

The panelling must have been rotten, and she had fallen through it. She looked upwards and then froze in terror.

Darkness . . . complete darkness. No chink of light to show how she came to be here. No gaping hole to show where she had broken through the panelling.

It was worse than her worst nightmares, because then a part of her had known she was dreaming. This was real.

Once, long ago, she had been imprisioned like this, beneath the stairs by her nanny. It had been Beatrice's fault. She had been the one to tell the nanny that Lucilla had disobeyed her orders and gone to her mother's room.

Cressida had been getting ready to go out. She had been angry with Lucilla for disturbing her. Lucilla could still remember her own feeling of bewilderment and unhappiness. She loved her mother so much, ached to be with her, spent hours daydreaming about it, but the reality always fell far short of her daydreams. In her dreams Cressida was never angry or impatient; and Beatrice wasn't there either, and she had had Cressida completely to herself.

Cressida had shouted at the nanny, and in retaliation she had locked Lucilla up in the cupboard under the stairs.

It had been a terrifying ordeal for a young child, and Lucilla had never forgotten it; because of it she had hated and resented Beatrice, blaming her for what had happened.

The nanny had left her there until after supper. Lucilla remembered that she hadn't cried when she had let her out, but she had screamed for weeks afterwards every time she was put to bed and her door shut.

In the end Beatrice used to come in and switch on her lamp for her, something that was expressly forbidden. Funny, she hadn't remembered that until now, and yet now she could quite clearly picture Bea's worried face and sad eyes. She had blamed Beatrice for what had happened, and yet in reality it had not been her fault. For the first time Lucilla wondered at the thoughtlessness of a mother who hadn't realised the torment suffered by her child.

Images flitted in and out of her mind as she sat in the cold darkness, fighting against the demons waiting to devour her, only just managing to hold her panic at bay.

Soon Nick would come and look for her and she would be safe. But what if he didn't? What if he simply thought she had left, and drove off? What if . . . ?

Sweat burst out of her pores, soaking her hairline, and yet at the same time she was frozen, the damp chill of the stone striking right through her flesh to her bones.

Something skittered in the darkness and she heard it. A scream welled up inside her, fear destroying reason as she screamed and beat her fists impotently against the walls of her prison.

She was a child again. Afraid and alone, and her fear was the fear of children the world over who know they are not loved, without knowing why . . . It echoed through her screams and was absorbed by the thickness of wood centuries old, unhearing and uncaring of the frantic demand of her fists beating against it.

Nick was more than half-way down the gallery.

He opened another bedroom door, expecting to confront Lucilla. The extent of his own simmering anger surprised him. He ought, after all, to have been prepared for what had happened last night, but he had thought he was beginning to establish a relationship with her, that she was beginning to accept him and to trust him, that she had begun to realise that with him there was no need for her to use and manipulate, the way she had other members of his sex. He had even been crazy enough to think that she was happy, that she accepted that she would never be an actress, but last night Benedict had shattered those foolish illusions by saying casually that Lucilla had told him that they were lovers.

He hadn't missed the element of spiteful malice in Benedict's smile when he had said the words, and he had derided himself for being as susceptible as the next man to male pride. He had thought himself beyond that kind of vulnerability, and he had been forced to admit to himself that he hadn't liked Lucilla's family looking upon him as just another victim in the long chain of men they had seen passing through her life.

Even so, instinctive need to protect Lucilla, even while he was infuriated with her, had stopped him from telling Benedict the truth.

Now, as he walked impatiently down the corridor, while the surface of his consciousness was irritated by the delay she was causing, at a deeper level he was still trying to come to terms with the depth of his response to her.

He had stood in the ballroom at the Grosvenor watching her; knowing her vulnerabilities and insecurities as though they were his own; knowing full well what she intended to do; knowing her reputation; knowing in fact everything there was to know about her. And in spite of it, as he looked at her, he had known that he loved her.

Love of that kind of intensity between a man and a woman had previously merely been an abstract ideal as far as he was concerned. There had been a couple of semi-serious relationships in his life—long-standing affairs involving mutual pleasure and affection—but he had never come anywhere near to experiencing what he was now feeling for Lucilla.

And yet, if he hadn't bought Max's agency, drawn back to the country where he had spent his teenage years, bonded to it in a way he had never been bonded to Hollywood, he would never have known her.

At the thought his footsteps quickened, his impatience tightening into a coiling, anxious sensation in the pit of his stomach.

Where the hell was Lucilla? He was well over half-way down the corridor now. The house was ideal, no doubts about it, but the whole venture had lost its gloss and become a sour taste in his mouth. He had actually been fool enough to believe that out of his own experience he could reach out to Lucilla, that . . .

He shook his head despairingly. He was thirty-five years old, for God's sake, and long past the age of being foolish enough to fall in love with a woman who could never be any of the things he wanted.

He had reached the last bedroom. He opened the door and surveyed its emptiness, his mouth tightening. If Lucilla was playing idiotic games . . . And then he noticed the leather bag she had been carrying. It was lying on the floor, its contents spewing out around it. He looked at the window-seat and frowned, unable to understand where Lucilla had gone, or why; and then he heard it, a thin, mewling sound that seemed to float toward him from behind the panelling.

Behind the panelling! He stared at it in shock.

He looked again at her handbag and studied the angle at which it had fallen. The window-seat, obviously. He touched the panelling experimentally and nothing happened.

He tried again, sweat dampening his skin, and wondered if he was over-reacting, but that thin, sharp cry had chilled his blood, and he was driven by a gut reaction to its terror stronger than any form of analytical logic.

He heard the click before he saw the panel move. It swung back sharply, giving him a brief glimpse of ancient stone before it closed again.

He opened it again, and was ready for it this

time, jamming it open with Lucilla's bag and his own coat. The light from the window illuminated a narrow flight of stone steps.

He wondered if he dared risk going down them, and decided that it was probably better not to.

Instead he called out sharply, 'Lucilla, are you there?'

The light had almost blinded her, it was so strong. Much stronger than she had expected, because the hall was narrow and dark. She had never liked the dark, but this had been worse that anything she remembered. It was cold under the stairs as well. She rubbed her hand over her eyes and then frowned.

It should have been Nanny who came to let her out, and not Elliott. Her half-brother should have been away at school.

'Lucilla!'

He was angry with her, she could hear it in the sharpness of his voice. She stood up, her legs wobbly. One of her knees hurt and she touched its warm stickiness experimentally. Nanny would be doubly cross now.

'Can I come out now?' she asked hesitantly.

Nick heard the quiet request and it chilled him. He could almost feel the hairs lifting on his scalp in atavistic apprehension. Even her voice was different—softer, more docile, like a child's.

A child . . .

'Yes, Lucilla, you can come out. You'll have to be careful on the steps, though. Can you manage them?'

'I think so.'

She sounded hesitant. Had she hurt herself?

That was funny . . . She didn't remember the cupboard having steps, but her head felt funny and woolly, and it was difficult to concentrate on anything for a long time.

She could see Elliott standing at the top of the steps, only he looked different somehow. She hesitated and blinked.

Nick felt the tension claw at his stomach muscles, locking them. Dear God, she was looking at him as though she had never seen him before.

'Elliott,' she said uncertainly.

He had no idea why she should think he was her half-brother, but he knew that it was vitally important that he shouldn't say or do anything to upset and alarm her, and dear God, he wanted her out of that hole so that he could see what damage she had done to herself. He couldn't go in after her without running the risk of the door shutting and locking them both in.

'Can you see my hand, Lucilla?' he encouraged softly. 'Get hold of it, there's a good girl, and then I can help you out. I can't come in, you see . . .'

'No, otherwise Nanny will lock you in as well,' she agreed docilely, shivering as Nick's fingers curled round her wrist and he almost dragged her the last few feet in his anxiety to have her safe.

There was a bruise on her forehead and she was filthy. She had been crying and there were black smudges of dirt on her face. Her tights were torn and one knee was bleeding slightly, but otherwise she seemed all right.

He looked at the bruise on her forehead and wondered if she was suffering from concussion. That might explain why she had confused him with Elliott, but the rest . . .

'I'm glad you're here, Elliott,' she told him shakily. 'You won't let Nanny put me back in the cupboard, will you?'

Nick stared at her. Her eyes were huge with fear and shock; wherever she was in her past, it was as real to her now as it must have been then, because this was no act. He thought quickly. The best thing he could do, the only thing he could do, was to simply allow her to believe he was Elliott. With any luck he could get her into the car and back with her family before anything too traumatic happened.

'No. No, I won't,' he reassured her. They were sitting on the window-seat and suddenly, to his shock, she edged toward him, pressing her body into the warmth of his. She was shivering violently, and he wrapped his arms around her, trying to comfort her with his own warmth.

'Promise . . . promise you won't let her do it.'

He drew a ragged breath and said huskily, 'I promise, Lucilla.'

She seemed reassured because the trembling subsided a little, and then, just as he was about to ease her away, she added inconsequentially, 'She was very cross with me.'

'Who? Nanny?'

She shook her head.

'No, Cressida . . .' She looked at him, and he

saw written clear in her eyes the misery and confusion of a hurt child. Her mouth wobbled as she told him, 'She said I was a nuisance and that she wished she'd never had me. She doesn't love me.'

The tears welled and trembled, and then splashed downwards; there was nothing he could do other than gather her into his arms and rock her comfortingly, stroking her hair.

Part of his brain told him that this was no time to simply sit there and hold her, that that bump on her forehead must signify some degree of concussion and that he should be rushing her to someone who could give her the proper medical attention; and yet another part, older and perhaps wiser, said that there would never be anything more important in their lives than what was happening now.

Under the confusion of her concussion, Lucilla was unlocking doors for him that he knew under normal circumstances she would never even have allowed him to guess existed.

He could have wept himself for the lonely misery of Lucilla as a confused child. He too had known that same fear and insecurity that went with being an unloved child, and yet in her siblings' eyes Lucilla was the one who had been their parents' favourite.

'Don't let Nanny lock me up again will you, Elliott?'

She looked up at him apprehensively and he stroked her hair, marvelling at its soft silkiness. Beneath it the bones of her skull felt frighteningly fragile.

He shuddered to think what could have happened to her if she had knocked herself out and not been able to call out, and suddenly, despite the beauty of the house, he wanted to get away from it.

'Promise me,' Lucilla demanded, clutching the front of his shirt.

'I promise,' he told her, bending to take her weight in his arms.

'Where are we going?'

She looked confused and wary.

'Somewhere nice, where you'll be safe and warm. It's cold here, isn't it?'

To his relief, she seemed to accept his words quite easily, nodding her head.

He noticed that by the time he had carried her down to the car her eyes were closed and she was breathing deeply.

He had a dim memory of reading somewhere that people suffering from concussion should not be allowed to sleep, so he shook her abruptly as he put her into the car. She opened her eyes and focused on him.

'Nick . . . How did I get here?'

He could see the panic hit her as she struggled to assimilate what was happening, and he urged, 'Don't worry, Lucilla. You've had a small accident. I'm taking you back to the house.'

'An accident . . . but how? Where? Nick, I can't remember . . .'

'You will,' he told her with more assurance than he felt. 'Just try to relax.'

He slid into the driver's seat and turned the key

in the ignition.

Later he decided that he had been extremely lucky not to come across any traffic police, because his Jaguar had responded to his need to get Lucilla home as quickly as possible, proving the excellence of a British car designed to cope with the irregularities of the British road system, with all its bends and sharp corners.

He didn't waste time once he stopped the car, sweeping Lucilla up into his arms, despite her protests.

Luckily, their arrival had been spotted. It was William who opened the door as they reached it, Beatrice hurrying down into the hall at his summons.

'Oh, Nick, what's happened?' she exclaimed worriedly.

'I'll explain later. Lucilla needs a doctor. Concussion,' he told her tersely.

Less than an hour later, Beatrice's GP closed Lucilla's bedroom door behind him and smiled reassuringly at the anxious waiting faces.

'You were right,' he told Nick. 'It is mild concussion. There's no fracture, fortunately, but she is exhibiting all the signs of someone suffering from deep shock.'

'Yes . . . yes, she will be, 'Nick agreed. 'I must admit I'm feeling rather shaky myself.'

'Look, let's all go downstairs and have a cup of tea,' Beatrice suggested. 'Then you can tell us exactly what happened.'

William, who had arrived unexpectedly mid-morning, offered to sit with Lucilla while the others went with the doctor, but the doctor assured them that he had given her a sedative and that she would be all right on her own.

'She'll be asleep by now,' he told them as they went downstairs and into Beatrice's own small sitting-room.

This was the room where she and Elliott relaxed when they were on their own. It was decorated in warm shades of peach, highlighted with white.

Pretty bookcases had been fitted either side of the fireplace and dragged in soft terracotta, and the squashy, comfortable sofa was upholstered in a patterned, polished cotton fabric that matched the curtains.

The hardwearing terracotta carpet had proved itself immune to spills from Dom's drinking cup, and Elliott considered that this room above all the others in the house reflected the warmth of his wife's personality.

William was despatched to make a pot of coffee, and while he was gone Nick started to explain what had happened.

He was able to describe his irritation at Lucilla's disappearance quite easily; he was even able to tell them how stunned he had been to realise that somehow Lucilla was trapped behind the panelling.

It was only when he started to describe finding her handbag that he realised that he had actually left it there, and William, coming into the room just as he was explaining how he had found the mechanism to open the panelling, said knowledgably, 'It must be a priest's hole of some sort. The house is the right age for it. Originally there was probably a passage leading from it to somewhere safe outside the house.

'Bedrooms were a favourite spot for priest's holes, but they normally put them behind the fireplace. I suppose when they were panelling the house, someone must have realised how easy it would be to construct a secret room. Poor Lucilla, it can't have been very nice being trapped in it.'

'She was petrified,' Nick told them slowly. He looked at their faces and felt like a traitor for what he was about to do, but they had to know the truth. The doctor would insist on knowing it, anyway. Nick suspected that he was already curious about the degree of shock Lucilla was suffering.

'I couldn't go into the room to get her out in case the door closed and we were both trapped. She thought I was you, Elliott.' He looked across the room and saw that Elliott was watching him intently.

'She'd reverted to her childhood. I don't know how old . . . four or five, perhaps . . . maybe even younger. She'd been locked away somewhere by her nanny . . .'

Beatrice made a small sound.

'She was barely four . . . Oh, Elliott, do you remember . . . that awful woman? She used to punish Lulu by locking her under the stairs.'

'Yes,' Elliott agreed harshly. 'I knew Lucilla was terrified of her, but I'd no idea why.'

'I only found out by accident,' Beatrice admitted. 'You know how we were never allowed to go into

Mother's room? Well, I saw her come in one day
and I wanted to tell her about something. I don't
remember what it was. The door was open and Lulu
was standing there. Miss Graham was holding on to
her arm trying to drag her away, but Lulu was
kicking and screaming. Mother was furious with
Miss Graham.

'I crept back upstairs, but Miss Graham never
brought Lulu back. And then I saw Mother go out
and get into her car, so I went down to look for Lulu.
I couldn't find her. I asked Miss Graham where she
was, and she said she was being punished for being a
naughty girl. She told me if I was naughty, I'd be
locked in the cupboard, too . . .'

Beatrice shivered. 'Oh, God . . . do you know, I'd
forgotten all about it? Oh, Elliott, how could we
have let that happen to her?'

'You could hardly have stopped it,' Elliott pointed
out to her drily. 'You were barely six yourself. And I
was away at school . . .' He frowned. 'Didn't Dad
sack Miss Graham?'

'Yes, I think he did. I remember Mother was
furious. She told him it was impossible to get good
staff.' Beatrice looked across at the doctor and said
uncomfortably, 'My mother was an actress. Her
career was very important to her.'

'Oh, such things aren't as uncommon as you
might think. Even these days,' the doctor told her
drily. He got up, and said to Beatrice, 'You'll find
your sister will probably sleep for the rest of today.
Tomorrow she'll probably feel slightly groggy. She
shouldn't need any further attention, but if you're at

all concerned give me a ring.'

'Oughtn't she to be in hospital . . . at least overnight?' Nick suggested anxiously.

'No. Her concussion was only very minor, and there are no signs that it's likely to develop into anything serious.'

After the doctor had gone, they all went back into the sitting-room. Beatrice looked shaken and pale.

'I had no idea. When I think of what she must have endured . . . How could Mother?'

She broke off and Elliott said grimly, 'Quite easily . . . Remember, Bea, that at the time your mother was a very unhappy woman herself. She still loved your father, and she was married to mine.'

'But she loved Dad Chalmers. She was happy with him.'

'After a fashion,' Elliott agreed, 'but with hind-sight I suspect that she might have resented Lucilla for being my father's child.'

'But Lucilla was always her favourite,' Beatrice protested.

Elliott raised his eyebrows.

'Was she? She was *Charles's* favourite . . .'

There was a small silence, broken only when William enquired hopefully, 'Isn't it time for lunch? I'm starving.'

It broke the tension. Beatrice got up, suddenly remembering that her son would be waking up from his nap.

Over her polished nut-brown head, Nick looked at Elliott and said quietly,

'I think I'll go up and sit with Lucilla, if you

don't mind.'

Beatrice turned her head and looked at him with dawning comprehension and said gently, 'Of course you can. I'll get Henry to bring you up a tray.'

Lucilla woke up later in the afternoon. She had the most appalling headache, and a sketchy, dim memory of the terror of her worst nightmare turning into reality.

Already it was going dark, and through the window she could see the gentle curves of the Cotswold hills.

She was at Bea's, of course. She closed her eyes thankfully, acknowledging an inner awareness that here she was safe, and then she opened them again, suddenly conscious of the man sitting beside her bed.

'Nick . . .'

He reached out across the bedspread and took her hand in his, and she was surprised to find that he was trembling slightly.

He had some papers spread out on the table in front of him. Lucilla couldn't understand what he was doing in her room, or even why she was in bed at this time of day, come to that, and yet she was conscious of something trembling just beyond the edge of her memory, something she didn't really want to remember. She shivered, before asking him, 'What are you doing here, Nick?'

'You had an accident . . . a fall. Don't you remember?' he asked her slowly.

She did . . . of course. A series of mental pictures

flashed through her mind. The panelled bedroom. Her argument with Nick. The window-seat. Her fall, and then that terrifying awareness that she was locked away in the darkness.

Her body began to tremble. Nick was still holding her hand; she tried to pull away.

The sound of the bedroom door opening startled them both.

Bea came in, her face clearing when she saw that Lucilla was awake.

'Oh, for heaven's sake, stop fussing, Bea,' Lucilla said irritably when Nick moved to one side to allow her half-sister to plump up her pillows.

She saw Nick's quick frown at her sharp words, and wondered forlornly what he would have said if he had known that her irritation sprang from the fact that Bea's arrival had prompted him to move away from the bed.

CHAPTER EIGHT

LUCILLA insisted on getting up to join the others for dinner.

Since the doctor had pronounced that she was not suffering from concussion there was no reason why she shouldn't, she snapped at Bea when the latter suggested it might be wiser for her to stay in bed.

Fully made-up, and wearing a dress that wouldn't have looked out of place in one of London's most glamorous eating spots, she went downstairs at half-past seven, looking just slightly paler than usual. Outwardly she looked poised and controlled. Inwardly she was petrified by the vague memories which had haunted her from the moment she had woken up: memories of hearing herself screaming, of darkness, of fear, of having in some terrifying way slipped back into the past and been a child again, no longer in control of her life, but subject to the will of others.

It was that terror and panic, that fear left over from the trauma of her childhood, that had made her get up rather than remain alone in her bedroom.

Elliott was dispensing pre-dinner drinks in the drawing-room when she walked in. His eyebrows rose slightly as he surveyed the elegance of her black dress, but he didn't remark on it, merely saying, 'I won't offer you anything alcoholic, Lucilla. It wouldn't be wise in view of the medication you've had. There's some spa water . . .'

Just for a moment Lusilla was tempted to demand a glass of dry sherry, but there had been times in the past when she had been tempted to cross swords with Elliott, and all too often they had ended in ignominy for her.

There might be times when she didn't particularly like her elder half-brother, but she always respected him.

'Very wise,' he murmured quietly, as he handed her her drink. She flashed him a bitter look, and then tensed. For the first time that she could remember, Elliott was looking at her with a mixture of the same compassion, concern and love that he normally reserved for his wife and son.

It sent her off balance, literally as well as figuratively; she felt herself sway slightly and become confused, the room blurring until she realised that the burning sensation in her eyes was caused by the tears that were obscuring her vision.

Tears? The mere thought of the humiliation she would suffer at betraying herself in such a way in front of her family sent a wave of icy dread through her body. She looked round desperately for some means of escape, and suddenly Nick was there, taking hold of her arm, reassuringly oblivious of the reason for her tension as he drew her slightly away from the others and started to talk to her.

It was several seconds before she had regained enough self-control to focus on what he was saying. He had drawn her towards the french windows and was saying something about the house they had visited.

She shuddered at the mere thought of it, but there was no denying that it would be ideal for filming purposes. When he said so, she agreed, keeping her face averted from him and praying desperately that the few tears she hadn't been able to control had not totally ruined her make-up.

'Here.'

The quiet word caught her attention.

'It's all right, no one's looking.'

She focused disbelievingly on the white cotton square he was holding out to her, and then raised her head and looked into his eyes.

He had known all the time what was happening to her. It hadn't simply been a fortuitous chance that he had drawn her away from the others.

Caught between chagrin and an odd, unfamiliar sense of relief that for once in her life she had someone else to rely on other than herself, she took the handkerchief and pressed it carefully to her damp face.

'It's just shock,' Nick told her calmly. 'Don't let it upset you.'

Shock. She shivered. He was right. She was suffering from shock, but not for the reason he had imagined. In that moment when she had looked at him and realised that he had deliberately tried to protect her, she had had the most shocking need to go into his arms, and be held there—safe, protected, cherished. All the things that no modern woman should ever want or expect from a man. All the things that she, who despised the male sex, knew they were incapable of providing.

Of course, there were exceptions . . . like Elliott.

'Ready to go back?'

Her panic made her overract.

'Of course,' she told him acidly. 'So much fuss about an eyelash in my eye.'

But she couldn't look at him, and all through dinner she was conscious of the corrosive fear burning inside her as she fought against the knowledge that had been born in that moment when she had wanted the physical warmth and reassurance of Nick's arms around her.

During dinner she barely took part in the conversation, and it was only when Nick mentioned his sister's name that she finally managed to divert her attention from her own thoughts and concentrate on what was being said.

'Of course, it was expected that both Sophy and I would play our parts in continuing the family tradition,' Nick was saying. 'Both of us appeared in a variety of films as kids. When I reached my teens the roles started to get fewer and fewer, until it began to dawn on me that I wasn't necessarily going to follow in my parents' footsteps.'

'That must have been a very difficult time for you,' Bea said sympathetically.

'Yes, it was, and it wasn't made any easier by the fact that Sophy was a natural. Both my mother and father were disappointed in me, but luckily I had our grandfather to turn to, or should I say my step-grandfather? He and my father had never really got on. He was a businessman, not part of the Hollywood scene, really, and I think my father had always resented the fact that his mother had remarried. She died when I was two or three, so I hardly remember her, but Gramps used to call by most days. Our folks were hardly ever there, and Gramps was really the only family we knew when we were growing up. I owe him a lot. He kept me sane when . . . when I needed keeping sane.'

'Living up to family traditions is never easy,' Elliott commented. 'We've had our fair share of suffering from that syndrome in this family.'

Lucilla tensed and glared at him, but before she could say anything Nick added pacifyingly, 'From what I've heard, Cressida and Charles were two very charismatic characters.'

'Well, that's one way of putting it,' Elliott drawled. 'In my opinion, though, their monumental selfishness was only modified by the fact that they were too immature to realise what they were. It's . . .

Beatrice looked uncomfortable, and touched Elliott's arm, trying to silence him, but to Lucilla's surprise she felt none of her normal fierce desire to leap to Cressida's defence. What was happening to her? Why was she changing like this? Or *was* she changing? Or simply stepping out from behind the image of her mother? It was a disconcerting thought.

At half-past nine Nick glanced at his watch and announced that it was time he left.

'I'll go and get my things,' Lucilla told him

absently. How odd that such a simple gesture should have such a powerful effect on her senses. That brief and very masculine movement of sinew and muscle; her sudden awareness of the very erotic contrast between hard, tanned flesh and soft, white cotton; these had bemused her so much that her verbal response had been entirely automatic, leaving her unprepared for Bea's concerned protest.

'She can't go back to London, Elliott,' she announced quickly. 'There's no one there to look after her. She must stay here . . .'

In the seconds that followed Lucilla was totally unaware of the look exchanged by Nick and Elliott, and conscious only of her own panicky reaction to Bea's suggestion, fuelled by the realisation that Nick could leave without her and that for some reason she didn't want to be parted from him.

To her relief she heard him saying calmly, 'She'll be all right,' reminding Beatrice, 'the doctor did say that there shouldn't be any after-effects.'

And yet, conversely, although she felt relieved that Nick had stopped Beatrice from pressing her to stay, she also felt ridiculously hurt that he was not more concerned about her.

It was an odd feeling for her to have, a naïve feeling in many ways, and if there was one thing she prided herself on it was not being naïve.

They left half an hour later, and they had reached the motorway before Lucilla had stopped seething over the way Nick had kissed Beatrice goodbye.

It struck her suddenly and explosively that she was jealous of her half-sister; that she had always been jealous of her. Jealous of Bea. Plain, dull Bea, who had always been the butt of Charles's humour and malice. Bea, who had never shown any inclination of developing any of the fabled Bellaire talent.

She felt so confused that she pressed her hands to her temples, trying to ward off the swirling thoughts that were threatening to sweep her away. Almost overnight her whole world had changed and become alarmingly unfamiliar, and as yet she wasn't sure of her footing in this new territory. Lucilla didn't like feeling alien and out of step; she liked to be in control of her life and everything in it.

'What's wrong?' Nick asked sharply, seeing her press her hands to her forehead.

'Nothing,' she told him shortly, lapsing into a moody silence. Surely she hadn't felt jealous of Bea because Nick had kissed her—an affectionate, friendly kiss, delivered in the presence of Bea's husband? And yet there had been a warmth in Nick's manner toward Bea that he had never shown her. Not even this evening when he saw her tears and gave her that handkerchief. But then, the circumstances of his first meeting with Bea were vastly different from his initial meeting with her. Bea had not been attempting to seduce his brother-in-law.

'I suppose you're another Elliott, and you think Bea is the epitome of everything that a woman should be, don't you?' she challenged abruptly.

She could feel Nick looking at her, even though she didn't turn her own head.

'I certainly think she's a very feminine and lovable woman,' he agreed calmly.

'Because she stays at home with her child, and doesn't have a thought in her head other than Elliott and Dominic? Of course, that would appeal to the male ego.'

'Not necessarily. A woman who elects to stay at home can be a dependent burden. You can't pigeon-hole people by their emotions, Lucilla. Look at my sister, for instance. When she and John got married, no one believed their marriage would last. Sophy is the image of our mother, and no doubt Hollywood thought John had got himself a bad bargain.' Lucilla looked at him, not sure what he meant.

'My mother was constantly unfaithful to my father,' he explained. 'She couldn't help herself. At least, that was her excuse. Normally her affairs didn't last, but just before they were killed she had asked my father for a divorce. He was flying the plane when it crashed. I've often wondered . . .'

Abruptly he went silent, and Lucilla's skin chilled despite the warm air circulating through the car.

'Do you mean that he killed them both rather than divorce her?'

'I don't know. What I do know is that he was a very proud man. It had been bad enough when . . . when he first discovered that she was unfaithful to him, but having turned a blind eye for all those years to those infidelities, and then to lose her . . . perhaps it was more than even he could take.'

Lucilla shivered again. An alien sense of loss and pain seemed to have entered the car; a mournful breath of long-ago emotions.

'He must have loved her very much.'

'No. I don't think he did,' Nick told her unexpectedly, 'but he had married her against all the advice of his family and friends, and he was the kind of man who would never admit to a mistake, so instead of ending the marriage as he should have done, he wasted the rest of his life blindly refusing to admit the truth, and in doing so he punished not only himself, but her as well, and to a lesser extent Sophy and me; in fact, everyone connected with them. He was not a happy man, nor an easy man to live with.'

'You didn't like him?'

'Not very much, although it was a long time before I was able to say that without guilt. It's normally love that bonds parent and child together, not liking, and without love, when there's no liking, it's a very difficult thing for a child to come to terms with. For years I struggled to be what I thought my father wanted me to be, always wondering why it was that nothing I did could please him. *I* loved him, you see . . .'

There was a long silence, and then Lucilla said huskily, 'Sometimes . . . sometimes I felt like that about Cressida. Oh, I know she loved me,' she added defensively. 'I was her favourite. But she was always so busy . . .'

She looked at Nick, and was surprised to see such a look of pity and compassion in his eyes that her throat closed up and she couldn't go on.

'Why are you looking at me like that? She *did* love

me . . .' She realised suddenly that she was practically screaming the words at him and that her fingers were curled into tight fists of tension.

Once before she had said those words, hurling them defiantly at Benedict. They had been quarrelling, she remembered, over something she had said to Bea. Ben had been about ten at the time. She had been fifteen, almost sixteen. Even now she could remember the way he had looked at her.

'She doesn't love you,' he had told her. 'How can she? You aren't a real Bellaire.'

She had sworn then that she would prove to him that she was more of a Bellaire than he would ever be, but she hadn't and he had been right. She wasn't a real Bellaire.

'Sometimes I hated her,' she said tiredly, the tension dropping sharply, leaving her feeling unreasonably weary. 'I did everything I could to make her notice me, but she was always too busy . . . or too involved with something else. I don't think she actually loved any of us.'

She could hardly believe she had really said the words. They seemed to hang in the silent atmosphere of the car, but instead of feeling guilt, she experienced a tremendous surge of release, of freedom from an almost intolerable burden.

The moment she uttered the words, she knew she had carried them inside her like a poisoned barb for a long time.

'Surprisingly easy, after all, isn't it?'

She looked uncomprehendingly at Nick.

'What?'

He gave her an oddly twisted smile, and said, 'Growing up. Welcome to the adult world, Lucilla Chalmers,' he added softly.

'Don't be ridiculous. I'm twenty-eight years old,' she scoffed irritably, 'and I've been an adult for almost a decade.'

'Legally, but not, I think, emotionally.'

Suddenly she felt too drained to pursue the subject. What was it about Nick that made her say and do these extraordinary things? In a matter of a few short weeks he had turned her whole world upside-down. She leaned back in her seat and closed her eyes, and didn't open them again until they were off the motorway and well into the city.

'So you think the house will do for the series?' she asked him sleepily as she sat up, and pushed her fingers through her mussed hair.

Suddenly it had become extremely important to her that she re-establish their business relationship and get away from personal matters.

'Yes, it will be ideal.' He looked at her. 'How will you feel about working there, though, after what happened?'

Her heart seemed to miss a beat. He was actually concerned about her, and then she realised that his concern was more likely to be in case she refused to work at the house, and not for her personally.

'No problem,' she told him coolly. 'After all, I'm hardly likely to be stupid enough to repeat the same mistake twice.'

She thought she heard Nick mutter under his breath, 'Oh, yeah?' but before she could challenge him he had turned off the main road and into an exclusive part of Chelsea where the road was only open to those people lucky enough to own one of the charming villas overlooking the Thames.

'I think it will be as well if you stayed here tonight. I promised Bea I'd take care of you,' he added before she could object, and then, when she remained frozen in her seat, he added bluntly, 'There's nothing to be afraid of, Lucilla. I'm not the kind of man who demands or wants sexual favours from unwilling women.'

'Don't be ridiculous,' Lucilla told him freezingly. 'I'm not afraid.' She almost scrambled out of the car in her haste to prove her point. She was, after all, supposed to be an experienced woman of the world, who would hardly balk at the thought of spending the night under the roof of a man who was known to her.

'Mrs Evans, who does for me once a week, always keeps the spare bed made up,' Nick told her as he ushered her inside.

The moment he said the words 'spare bed', Lucilla told herself she was a fool for ever imagining he could have meant anything different. After all, if he wanted to make love to her he could have done so the first time they met.

But he hadn't known her then . . . not really known her. And, as the thought formed, it hurt to realise that knowing her had not altered his opinion of her, or his lack of desire for her. And that last little piece of knowledge stopped her in her tracks.

For the first time in her life, Lucilla really knew

what it was to experience the pain of sexual rejection.

'Lucilla, are you all right?'

Nick turned abruptly in the narrow hall to study her. Before she could stop him he lifted her wrist, circling it with strong fingers, his thumb touched her now racing pulse.

'The doctor said no after-effects,' he muttered to himself. 'God, perhaps I should have left you with Bea and Elliott, after all,' he added broodingly, searching her pale face.

'No, no . . . I'm fine,' Lucilla told him. 'Just a bit tired. Nick . . . I'd prefer to go home. I'll be all right . . .'

'No way,' he told her forthrightly. 'You're staying here. Come on. I'll take you up to your room. You'd better go straight to bed.'

'But we've got work to do.'

'Nothing that won't wait until tomorrow.'

It was oddly comforting simply to give up and let him take charge, to follow him into the pretty lemon and white guest bedroom with its own tiny bathroom, and to listen obediently while Nick told her that she was to get into bed and he'd bring her up a hot drink.

For someone who had always claimed that she enjoyed living alone, it was strangely comforting to be able to hear Nick moving about downstairs while she prepared for bed. Presumably her bedroom was over the back of the house and the kitchen area. She was in bed when he came back. He hesitated for a moment in the doorway, an unfathomable look on his face, and Lucilla realised, touching her face self-consciously, that she was without her usual make-up. Up until that moment she hadn't given a thought to the fact that Nick would be seeing her without her usual protective gloss. He was, in fact, the first male outside her family with whom she had shared anything approaching that particular kind of intimacy.

Her heart gave an odd lurch, and she felt as shy and self-conscious as a sensitive teenager.

'For goodness' sake, stop staring at me,' she protested waspishly. 'I can't be the first woman you've seen in bed.'

It was a pretty feeble attempt at her normal brittle sophistication, but it seemed to work. Nick walked over to the bed and put down the tea he had brought her.

'I'm going to ring Bea and let them know you'll be staying here for a few days, to put her mind at rest.'

As the door closed quietly behind him, several thoughts struck her at the same time.

The first and most powerful was a bewildering sense of loss, an aching pain inside that made her want to cry out to him to come back and stay with her.

The second was her angry recognition of her own selfishness in not being the one to suggest ringing Bea, and the third was a searing, burning jealousy of her elder sister, mixed with anguish that Nick's concern for her might simply be a by-product of his greater concern for Bea, and that it might be simply to protect and help Bea that he was insisting she stayed with him.

Nick, in love with her sister? Impossible, surely. Or was it?

She picked up the sturdy mug Nick had brought her. So different from her own translucent modern china, and yet somehow comforting to hold, the heat of the tea warming her hands.

She drank it quickly and then settled back in bed. Within minutes she was deeply asleep.

Downstairs, Nick replaced the receiver and then went slowly upstairs. Lucilla was asleep, impossibly dark lashes fanning her pale cheeks. Like this, she looked frail and vulnerable. It was almost impossible to imagine how swiftly her eyes could chill and glitter, and how bitter and venomous that soft mouth could be.

All in self-defence, and all heart-breakingly unnecessary. He reached out and carefully tucked an errant blonde lock behind her ear. The weekend had drained him, and yet at the same time he felt elated. For the first time he felt as though he was really getting through to her, making her see how distorted her vision of her past and her family actually was. Out of need and love she had clung to her own images of Cressida and Charles, setting them both up on pedestals.

But now those pedestals were crumbling. He looked broodingly at her sleeping form, impelled by a sudden urge to wake her and take her in his arms, to force her to realise how right they were for one another, to make love to her and awaken the real

woman he knew lay slumbering beneath her
protective brittleness. But he couldn't do it. It
wouldn't be fair to her, and in the end it wouldn't be
fair to himself, either. No. She must come to him
willingly, loving him, or not at all. Patience . . .
Patience was the key, but there were times when he
ached to ignore the cool commands of his brain and
give in instead to the fierce ache of his body.

He bent and dropped a light kiss on her forehead.
In her sleep, she smiled.

He felt the heat flood his skin, his body painfully
aroused by his need to make love to her.

Turning abruptly, he left the room.

CHAPTER NINE

'BUT, Nick, I never eat breakfast.'

'Then you should.'

They were sitting in the small, pretty dining-room just off the kitchen, Nick presiding over the coffee-pot with a deftness that did nothing to detract from his masculinity.

He had walked into her room less than an hour ago, carrying a cup of tea, and had been surprised to find her awake and keen to get up. At first he had tried to persuade her to spend the day resting, but Lucilla had organised a tentative lunch meeting with Tracy Hammond and there was no way she was going to miss it.

'I'm perfectly well,' she had insisted, and, although it was true in one sense, in another it was not. She felt decidedly off balance: ill at ease with herself and acutely aware of how much a strain it was becoming to keep up her normal aggressive, cynical attitude of self-sufficiency and control.

Lying awake in Nick's spare bed this morning, it had come to her for the first time that, in many ways, all her life she had been playing a role. Now she was making the first tentative explorations of her own real self. It was rather like looking at her reflection in a mirror, and then discovering that the reflection was real and independent, and she found it disconcerting to discover how easy it was to slip into her now softer, more relaxed persona.

Some elements of the old Lucilla still remained, though, and one of them was her total aversion to the thought of food before twelve o'clock, but Nick was adamant, which was why she was pushing a small slice of toast round an earthenware plate that matched the mug of coffee he had just poured her.

In actual fact she was glad of the toast, because it gave her something to concentrate on other than the broad expanse of Nick's chest, warmly tanned against the stark whiteness of his towelling robe.

'Eat it,' he told her, adding succinctly, 'No breakfast, no lunch.'

Lucilla scowled at him.

'I'm not a child, Nick.'

'Then stop behaving like one,' he told her promptly. 'You need to eat, Lucilla. You're too thin.'

She opened her mouth to object, but before she could stop him he had practically lifted her out of her chair, pushing her fashionably bulky sweater out of the way, to hold her waist within the span of his hands.

The heat of the skin-on-skin contact where his fingertips touched her middle unnerved her. She began to panic, trying to free herself.

'What's wrong?' Nick asked quietly.

He was so close to her that she had to tilt her head back to look at him.

'I'm cold.'

The rash of goose-bumps on her skin where he

was touching her seemed to prove her claim, and he released her slowly, gently pulling her sweater back into place. Shivering slightly, she sat down and reached for her coffee, praying that she was the only one of them who knew that those tiny bumps had been caused by the unfamiliar friction of his touch against her skin and her body's reaction to it.

'Hadn't you better get dressed?'

She said the words without looking at him, and could have bitten out her tongue. Would he guess how much his state of near nudity was disturbing her? The bathrobe covered him from knee to throat more or less, but she was acutely aware of the warmth of his skin and her own realisation that he was most probably naked underneath it.

To her relief he took her comment at face value and grimaced, 'Slave driver, but I suppose you're right.' He turned toward the door, and added warningly, 'And eat that toast. The next thing we know you'll be wanting a dog so that you can feed it under the table.'

Lucilla was stunned. Just for one brief, shocking instant his words had conjured up a mental image of the kind of domestic harmony she had always thought was the province of the Beas of this world; the kind of life she had always insisted was not for her.

She looked down at her plate and realised she had actually eaten the toast, and what was more she had enjoyed it. She took another slice and spread butter on it thinly.

From upstairs, Nick called down, 'Make some

fresh coffee, will you? I can't even begin to think of functioning in the morning without half a dozen cups.'

If it was an exaggeration, it was only a slight one, Lucilla realised an hour later when they were eventually ready to set out for the office.

Nick, to her astonishment, had insisted on clearing away the breakfast things and then washing up, explaining that Mrs Evans, his cleaner, only came in once weekly, and that he preferred to take care of himself.

Lucilla had actually found herself drying crockery for the first time since she had left her childhood behind her. And yet there had been a comfortable contentment in sharing the mundane chore.

It struck her when they were in Nick's car that she wasn't looking forward to going back to her own flat, but go back she must. She said as much as Nick parked.

'Not yet,' he told her abruptly. 'That was some fall you had, Lucilla. It would be much more sensible to stay with me. In fact, I'm going to insist upon it. We've got one hell of a lot to get through in the next few weeks, and it will be much easier if you're there on the spot, so to speak.'

She ought to have objected, to have insisted on returning to her own home, but the thought of doing so was totally unappealing, and she found herself weakly agreeing to allow Nick to drive her home later so that she could collect some clothes.

Lucilla had a busy morning dealing with an

avalanche of telephone calls following the official Press releases concerning the new series. Nick had been quoted as being the main casting agent, and his relationship with John Cassavar had been mentioned in several of the theatrical papers.

Lucilla's lunch with Tracy Hammond had been arranged by the latter's agent. Lucilla had spoken to him the previous week, and, although he had told her that Tracy had an extremely busy schedule, he had nevertheless been interested enough to arrange the lunch.

'Tracy is a serious actress,' he had warned Lucilla. 'She isn't interested in taking any soap roles.'

'This one's different,' Lucilla had told him, and that was exactly what she intended to tell the young actress. She was determined to sell the role to her, because she sincerely believed that Tracy was right for it.

It amazed Lucilla herself how much pleasure and self-satisfaction she was getting from her new career. Much more than she had ever had from her old, if that could actually be called a career.

The restaurant arranged for the meeting was a popular one.

When Lucilla walked in and was shown to the actress's table, she discovered that there were already several people there and her heart sank a little. She had hoped to talk to Tracy alone.

Her heart sank even further when she saw Benedict, but Sebastian was also with him. Sebastian had a calming, softening effect on his older twin, and this might be a golden opportunity to persuade Sebastian to test for the part of Kit Weston.

She sat down beside him, having introduced herself to Tracy. The actress was was busy talking to someone else, and Lucilla wanted to wait until she had her full attention before discussing the part with her.

Lucilla had always felt slightly more at ease with Sebastian than with the rest of her family. He had a gentleness none of the others seemed to possess, and she welcomed it now as he asked her how her new job was going.

'I like it,' she told him candidly, breaking off as she realised that Tracy was now sitting on her own. Excusing herself to Sebastian, she went over to sit with her.

Half an hour later, to her elation, she had got Tracy's tentative agreement to test for the role, and she felt confident that once Tracy realised how seriously the whole thing was being treated her reservations would disappear.

Elated and pleased with herself, she went back to sit with Sebastian, who had now finished his main course.

'Success?' he asked her.

'I hope so. She's perfect for Tabitha. Which reminds me . . . there's a part in it which would be perfect for you.'

Quickly she outlined the plot.

Sebastian frowned.

'But surely, ideally, Ben would be better playing

Kit than me.'

'No, I don't think so. The character of Kit requires a great deal of depth, Sebastian. On the surface, yes, he's a charmer—feckless and slightly reckless, but inside . . . he needs to be played by someone who can portray those deeper qualities. Ben's too like the surface Kit to do that.'

'Well, well, now our failed actress is an expert at character analysis as well as everything else.'

Lucilla tensed but didn't turn her head to look at Benedict. How long had he been standing behind her, listening? What did it matter? She had only spoken what she considered to be the truth.

'Poor Lucilla, you must be quite exhausted. Working all day . . . as well as all night.'

It was said just loud enough for everyone to hear.

Sebastian frowned.

'Ben . . .'

'Oh, come on. You know as well as I do that the only way Lucilla's ever got anyone to employ her is by lying . . .'

Lucilla slapped him, shocking herself as much as she shocked him.

'You always were a venomous little bitch,' Benedict snarled at her, nursing the flaming marks on his face. 'Venomous and jealous as hell of the rest of us because you aren't really a Bellaire.'

'Ben, stop this!' Sebastion protested, but his twin ignored him, pushing off his restraining arm to say angrily,

'Well, you and Barrington make a good pair.

Rumour has it he would have as little right to the Barrington name as you have to the Bellaire.'

'Ben, that's not true,' Sebastian warned. 'You're just repeating Hollywood gossip.'

'There's never any smoke without fire,' Benedict returned. 'It was all round Hollywood at one time that his mother played around. The day he was born, Silas Barrington refused to even look at him. he even cut him out of his will, but your lover still hung on to the Barrington name, just as you've hung on to the Bellaire name.'

The whole table had fallen silent, fascinated by what was going on. Sebastian looked uncomfortable and embarrassed, but Lucilla was only peripherally aware of other people's reactions.

All her concentration was focused on Benedict as she stood up and said firmly, 'Nick would have been a success whatever name he chose to use, because he's that kind of man. I don't give a damn who his father was or wasn't. Do you know something, Ben? You were right, I *was* jealous . . . bitterly so, but not any more.

'You can keep the Bellaire name and everything that goes with it, and I pity you for having to do so.' She turned to Tracy Hammond and said calmly, 'I'll be in touch about the arrangements for the test.' And then she looked at Ben and said quietly, 'I hope that one day someone will open your eyes to reality the way mine have been opened. Being a Bellaire means nothing.'

'You think that now,' Benedict sneered. 'Wait until Barrington kicks you out. You'll sing a different song then.'

Lucilla didn't wait to hear any more. She smiled at Sebastian and, with her head held high, walked out of the restaurant.

She didn't go back to the office, but instead took a taxi home.

Once inside her own house, she went straight up to her bedroom and opened the wardrobe doors.

An hour later she rang Bea and announced, 'I've been having a sort through my clothes. There's tons of stuff here I want to get rid of. Any suggestions?'

Beatrice had, and, having made arrangements for her things to be collected, Lucilla replaced the receiver and then redialled.

Sometimes it was rather pleasant being an independently wealthy woman. Her father's money might not have been able to buy her acting success, but it did have its uses.

If the interior designer she telephoned was startled by the magnitude of her commission, she gave no sign of it. Lucilla knew nothing of her other than that she specialised in soft, pretty, chintzy effects pepped up to fit into a city environment.

She replaced the receiver and gave a satisfied glance around the room.

All she needed to do now was to go out and buy some new clothes, and then the transformation would be complete.

Although the shops she visited pointed out slightly severely that late November was not the time to be purchasing an autumn wardrobe, Lucilla was very pleased with what she managed to achieve.

Soft cashmeres in colours that stopped just short of being sugar-almond sweet; fabrics that draped and clung in a feminine rather than a sexual fashion; high-heeled shoes that emphasised the delicacy of her ankle bones. And, to complete her new look, softer, prettier make-up.

She left Harvey Nichols at half-past four, dressed from head to foot in new clothes, wearing new make-up and carrying far too many glossy carrier bags.

The taxi dropped her just outside the office, and by the time she had reached their office floor she was beginning to feel the effect of her exertions.

The receptionist goggled slightly at the sight of her parcels, and Lucilla returned her look with an almost urchin grin.

She almost danced into her office, light-headed with sensations that ranged from exhilaration to relief.

She was just taking off her coat when the door was flung open and Nick walked in.

'Lucilla, where the hell . . .' He broke off as he took in her new appearance.

'Hello,' Lucilla said gravely, holding out her hand to him. 'I'm Lucilla Chalmers.'

He was not appeased. In fact, if anything, he looked even more grimly angry than he had been before.

'For God's sake, Lucilla! Have you any idea how worried I've been? You disappear for damn near three hours without a word . . . But than, that's you all over, isn't it? Selfish, thoughtless. Never thinking of anyone other than yourself . . .'

This was the second time he had been angry with her. Her new self-confidence evaporated and she took refuge behind a cool wall of mock-indifference, shrugging her shoulders and saying mockingly, 'You aren't my keeper, Nick. Or did you think that just because I work for you that you've got exclusive rights to me?'

It was the kind of loaded sexually taunting comment she would have once made without thought. Now its effect on Nick made her insides quiver.

He looked at her with corrosive contempt and said quietly, 'What man could ever think that?' And then he walked out.

The temptation to sit down at her desk and bury her head in her arms and burst into tears was almost too great to resist, but she was glad that she had, because within minutes Nick was back, carrying a heavy briefcase.

'Come on. We're going home,' he told her curtly.

Going *home?* After what they had just said to one another?

If she had any pride she would walk out on him right now, but she was coming to realise that, where Nick was concerned, pride was of no importance. She wanted to be with him; she wanted to be part of his life, part of him, in a way that had nothing to do with anything she had ever experienced before.

She loved him, she realised with a small shock of sensation. She stared unfocusingly at her desk. How could that have happened? *When* had it happened?

She walked across the room to pick up her parcels, and found suddenly that she was shaking.

'God, I knew something like this would happen. That damned doctor! He ought at least to have taken you into hospital for surveillance.'

She was pushed out of the way while Nick gathered up her purchases.

'And you should have had more sense. What on earth possessed you . . . Haven't you got enough damn clothes already?

'No,' Lucilla told him quietly. 'All the ones I had belonged to Lucilla Bellaire.'

Now she had his attention. Now he looked at her. Now he saw the soft femininity of her cashmere dress and the way it fitted her body, the soft make-up, and the hesitant, almost shy look in her eyes.

He dropped the parcels and his briefcase.

'Oh, God, Lucilla.'

She was in his arms, feeling the heavy, uneven thud of his heart. Her own sang. She wound her arms round him, shivering in delicious pleasure as she heard his low groan of desire. His hands were in her hair, stroking through its silky length. His lips touched her forehead and she quivered in response. For the first time in her life she wanted a man to touch her, to make love to her. All the provocative, deliberately sensual gestures and movements she had used in pursuit of ambition deserted her, leaving her with no way of showing him what she felt other than to press her body into the muscled hardness of his, aching to have his mouth on hers, and yet totally unable to lift her head and initiate the kiss herself.

But then, as she felt him pull away from her, despair made her inventive and she raised herself up on tiptoe and whispered softly, 'I'm sorry. I didn't mean to worry you.' And then she placed her mouth on his in a kiss of peace.

Nick froze. The temptation to part the softly closed line of her mouth and kiss her as he had been aching to do since that first night burned inside him. He could feel her breasts pressing against him, and it was only with the greatest effort of will that he was able to stop his body from betraying him.

Lucilla looked at him, her eyes betraying her confusion and humiliation. She stepped back from him and drew a shuddering sigh.

Nick couldn't stand it. Just for a moment he had seen in the vulnerability of her eyes the Lucilla he had always know was there. The Lucilla he had fallen in love with. He made a harsh sound in his throat, and said huskily, 'I'm sorry, too.'

And then he was kissing her. Really kissing her, Lucilla realised, as his mouth probed hers.

His hand cupped her jaw, his thumb stroking her lower lip. Lucilla was bemused by the sensations such a light caress caused. She could actually feel her breasts swell and the nipples harden while her lips softened, sensitised by his touch. She could hardly breathe, and she had to open her mouth to drag in air. She realised that the harsh sound she could hear was Nick's unsteady breathing, and she lifted her bemused gaze to meet his.

'Kiss me again, Nick.'

She could hardly believe she had said the words, hardly believe that that husky little appeal came from her.

It had, though. Already Nick was responding to her plea, bending his head, so that his breath feathered tormentingly against her mouth as he whispered, 'How? Like this?'

He was teasing her mouth with his, tormenting it with light, butterfly kisses that only teased its parted moistness.

She was actually trembling in his arms, clinging despairingly to him as she shook her head, desperate to convey to him her need.

At last he seemed to realise, because he stopped tormenting her and asked softly, 'Not like that? How, then? Show me.'

Show me. The words shocked through her, and she stared at him in consternation, and then her glance dropped to his mouth and she shuddered in the grip of her intense need, pressing her mouth hesitantly to his as she had done before, but this time the bonds of restraint she had always imposed on herself snapped, and with a little cry of desperation she pressed pleading kisses against his mouth, until it opened and she could taste him properly.

Her soft, satisfied sound of pleasure broke his self-control. His hands found her breasts and shaped their rounded contours. Lucilla moaned in arousal and discovered that she had lost control of the kiss, but she didn't mind. And then, somewhere in an outer room, a door banged and Nick released her abruptly, bending awkwardly, retrieving his briefcase and her parcels.

'Nick . . .'

'Not now, Lucilla. Let's get home first, where we can talk privately.'

Home . . . Her heart sang. Home for her would always be with Nick.

Funny how she knew that and accepted it, even welcomed it. She who had always wanted her independence. She floated out to the car on a wave of euphoria.

CHAPTER TEN

SOMEWHERE on the way back to Nick's Chelsea house, her euphoria died. Or was it the oppressive silence emanating from Nick—so at odds from his mood when he kissed her—that killed it?

Lucilla only knew that, by the time they were eventually inside the house, she was bitterly regretting her foolishness in kissing him, and was tensing herself against the pain of him making some sardonic remark about both the kiss and her changed appearance. But he said nothing other than a curt, 'I've got to ring the States. Sophy will be wanting to know how we're getting on with finding her somewhere to live.'

They had lined up several possible houses to view over the weekend, and it came as a shock to Lucilla to hear Nick saying tersely, 'I think it might be a good idea if you viewed them on your own. I've got rather a backlog of work to catch up on, and if John does decide to reschedule the filming to fit in with Tracy Hammond's commitments, I'll need everything else out of the way.'

Unthinkingly, Lucilla protested, 'But I can't view the houses on my own, Nick.'

'Then ask Bea,' Nick tole her brusquely. 'She'll probably be willing to help.'

Of course Bea would help, but Lucilla hated

feeling that Nick was comparing her abilities to her half-sister's and finding her wanting, and she reacted instinctively to her jealousy, saying bitterly, 'I've got an even better idea—why don't you simply ask Bea to take over the whole thing? I'm sure she'd prove to be a much better assistant than me,' she finished sarcastically.

'Very probably,' Nick agreed harshly, silencing her. 'One thing's for sure, she'd certainly prove to be a far less troublesome one.'

He said the words half under his breath, but Lucilla heard them and immediately leapt to the conclusion that he was regretting the impluse which had led to him giving her the job in the first place.

What had happened to the man who had kissed her in his office? Why was Nick behaving like this with her, as though he wanted her out of his life just as quickly as it could be arranged?

Lucilla wasn't a fool; she had witnessed too many men trying to rid themselves of women they no longer wanted to be deceived. Nick regretted kissing her, he didn't want the intimacy with her that the kiss they had shared had been a prelude to, and rather than tell her outright he was trying to backpedal and push her into being the one to make the break between them. She had seen it happen so often before and despised the man involved for his weakness, but she had never dreamed Nick, of all people, would behave in such a way.

If he didn't want her, all he had to do was to simply tell her so. Didn't he have enough respect for her, enough liking, enough compassion even to be honest with her?

She wanted to be angry with him, to despise him as she had despised so many other members of his sex, but all she could feel was a hurting, burning pain in the region of her heart and an insane desire to burst into tears.

She loved him, something she had never imagined she would ever do; and almost as soon as she had discovered her love, she had also discovered the pain that came with knowing that her feelings weren't shared or returned. But at least she had enough pride left not to beg or cling. Nick had made it plain that he didn't want her. The least she could do for both of them was to accept his rejection.

'Well, if you've got things to do, I'll go up to my room and put this lot away.'

She turned her back on him as she picked up up parcels. She thought she had given a very good impression of calm indifference, but obviously something must have given her away because behind her, she heard Nick saying with rough exasperation, 'Oh, hell, Lucilla. Look . . .'

He swore as the phone rang, but picked up the receiver.

Lucilla carried on collecting her parcels, and as she walked through the open door into the hallway, she heard him saying, 'Sophy, hi! No, I'm sorry we haven't found you anywhere yet, but Lucilla has a few hopefuls to look at this weekend.'

She went upstairs to her small, pretty room, but,

instead of unpacking her purchases, she gathered together her other belongings.

Odd, disjointed thoughts whirled through her head. She would never know now whether or not she had been successful in persuading Tracy to take the role of Tabitha. She wouldn't be instrumental in finding Sophy a house. She would, in fact, have no connection with the film at all . . . or with Nick.

It was fortunate that she wouldn't need, *didn't* need to earn her own living. Who would employ her—a failed actress-cum-agent with nothing to recommend her other than a rather dubious talent for persuading a certain kind of man to behave even more idiotically than nature had intended?

She had no illusions about herself now. She could have made a success of this job; she knew it instinctively. With Nick at her side she could have learned to balance the disparate pieces of her life; she could have found happiness. But it was not to be . . . Nick himself had made that clear.

She left quietly while he was still on the telephone.

The taxi driver she found cruising past the end of the mews made no comment when he saw her suitcase and her white face. Break-ups of relationships were too common to warrant any reaction these days.

Her own house felt cold and empty, the strident décor striking discordant notes on her emotionally raw nerve-endings. She would have to find some temporary accommodation. The interior designer and her team were due to start on Monday. Perhaps

Elliott and Bea . . .

Funny how she always ran home to her half-sister when things went wrong.

She glanced at her watch. By now, Nick would probably have realised she had gone. He would be relieved, of course, that she had been so quick off the mark. Another woman might have stayed to plead or argue, to demand an explanation of that passionate kiss followed so quickly by that brusque indifference, but she was not as gullible as the majority of her sex.

She might not be a good actress herself, but she was a expert at picking up on people's body language, and Nick's had told her quite plainly how much he regretted kissing her.

One kiss, that was all, and yet it had opened her eyes to so much—her own love for Nick for one thing.

Deep in thought, she didn't hear the car outside, or the front door opening. Her first intimation that she wasn't alone any longer came when Nick said abruptly behind her, 'Just what the hell are you playing at?'

She whirled round, too stunned to hide her reaction.

'How did you get in here?'

He dangled a bunch of keys in front of her.

'You left these in the front door. For God's sake, Lucilla, have you gone completely out of your mind? Do you know what the crime rate is in London? Not to mention the rape statistics.'

'I don't know why you followed me here, Nick,

but I'd like you to leave. Like you, I've got rather a busy evening planned. Although my evening will be busy in a different context,' she told him with a hard laugh.

'You think so? Well, whatever you've got planned you can just forget it. You're coming back with me.'

'Why?' Lucilla demanded baldly. 'So that you can shut me in my bedroom while you get on with your work?'

His mouth thinned.

'You can argue all you like,' he told her harshly. 'But you're coming back.'

'Make me,' Lucilla challenged him dangerously.

'Oh, I will . . . with pleasure!'

Of course, it would be her luck that there wasn't a single person in the street outside to witness Nick's cavalier disposal of her objections as he carried her out of the house and dumped her in his car, ignoring her demands to be put down.

He even locked her in the car while he went back inside to collect her still unpacked suitcase and lock her front door behind him.

'God-awful décor,' he muttered balefully, as he got into the car and slammed the driver's door.

'I happen to like it,' Lucilla lied.

'Oh, yeah?' He turned his head to give her an acid look. 'What happened to the new image . . . the softer, more feminine woman?'

Inside she bled with pain, but she hid it from him. That had been no mere image—that had been her first fumbling step toward the woman she suspected she really was, the woman she could become if he only had the love and patience to help her, but he hadn't, and so she shrugged and said with acid sweetness, 'Well, it certainly fooled you.'

They exchanged a long look, bitter with mutual hostility and anger.

'Only for a very brief space of time,' Nick told her harshly.

After that, neither of them spoke. Lucilla had no idea why Nick was insisting on her returning to his house. She would have thought he would have been only too glad to take the way out she had offered him.

She ought to be talking to him right now about her resignation, she ought to be telling him that there was no way she was going to spend another night under his roof, but she was too numb, too exhausted by own emotions to do anything.

When he stopped the car, Nick took a firm grip on her arm, almost marching her into the house.

There were papers scattered liberally over the sitting-room floor, evidence of the way he must have rushed out to find her. Someone else looking at this room might have seen in its disorder a lover's impatience, but how wrong they would be!

'I'm hungry,' Lucilla announced arrogantly. The more obnoxious she was, the more likely Nick was to stop this charade of taking responsibility for her, but he ignored the challenge of her words and said equably, 'So am I. I'll clear this lot up and make us something to eat.'

Although she had told herself she wasn't going to

help him, Lucilla found herself drifting into the kitchen to watch him as he prepared their meal. He was cooking steak and had removed a bowl of salad from the fridge.

Lucilla examined it. It was rather dreary. She opened cupboard doors, found what she was looking for and set out to pep it up.

She realised that Nick had stopped what he was doing to watch her.

'Odd how domesticity appears to suit you,' he said grimly. 'Quite the chameleon, aren't you?'

His gibe hurt, her appetite suddenly deserting her. She banged the salad bowl down on the counter and walked out of the kitchen.

By the time she had reached her bedroom, she was shaking, her face wet with tears. She went into her bathroom and locked the door behind her, turning on both taps and shower so the noise would drown the awful, racking sobs convulsing her.

Outside Nick banged on the bathroom door, but she ignored his demand that she open it.

She wanted to die, to simply close her eyes and disappear. She hadn't known when she was best off. The old Lucilla would never have suffered like this. *She* hadn't been capable of such suffering. The new Lucilla was all too capable of it, too vulnerable, too weak, too much in love.

When she eventually stopped crying, she looked in the mirror. Her eyes were red and puffy, her expression so unfamiliar that she could hardly believe the reflection staring back at her was hers.

It took almost half an hour to bring down the

swelling with cold water and cotton wool.

When she eventually dried her face and opened the bedroom door her bedroom was in darkness, and then she saw the tray on the dressing-table.

She switched on the lamp.

Under the cling film was her salad, and on the tray was a thermos of coffee. She poured herself a cup, wondering if Nick would come back upstairs. The salad she didn't touch. She wasn't hungry.

Common sense told her to go downstairs and talk to Nick, to explain to him coolly and firmly that it would be more sensible for her to return to her own home, but she wasn't sure she could do it without either bursting into tears or flinging herself into his arms, and so she took what she considered to be the coward's way out and showered and then crawled into bed.

She didn't expect to sleep; her mind was in too much of a turmoil, but surprisingly she did, half waking briefly with the sensation of struggling to free herself from some unknown terror, which her half awake brain vaguely realised belonged to a nightmare. But before she could, sleep again claimed her, the nightmare sucking her down into its black depths, the terror of her incarceration in the cupboard rising up to claim her so that she threshed wildly in the bed and screamed her panic.

Nick took the stairs three at a time, pushing open the bedroom door and reaching her bedside just as her own scream roused her from her sleep.

'Lucilla, it's all right. It's all right . . .'

'It was the cupboard,' she whispered, still caught

up in her dream.

'Yes, I know.'

She looked into his face and saw that he did, and she froze.

How can you? No one knows . . .'

'No, Lucilla,' he corrected her. 'I know. Elliott knows, and so does Bea. When you fell through the panelling, you were trapped. Don't you remember?'

Suddenly she did, and she shuddered, recalling her terror.

'When I got you out, you thought I was Elliott. You talked about your nanny and being punished by being locked in a cupboard.'

He saw how stiff and tense she was, and said quietly, 'It's all right, Lucilla. You're safe now.'

'Now,' she agreed bitterly, not looking at him, but back into the past. 'But not then. I told my mother, but she wouldn't believe me. She didn't want to believe me, just like she didn't want to be bothered with me. I was a nuisance . . . a child she didn't want by a man she didn't love.'

She was so tense, he could feel the rigidity in her bones as he cradled her against him in his arms.

'It's all right, Lucilla. It's over . . .'

'It will never be over . . . never!'

'Because you won't let it. Do you think you're the only child to suffer the pain of parental rejection?'

He had her attention now. She focused on him, the frightening blankness dying from her eyes, but he knew he had to go on talking to stop her from drifting back into her past.

'My rejection wasn't the same, but it was there, none the less. Sophy was always my father's favourite. I grew up knowing that, but accepting it, until one day I heard my mother's friends gossiping, and I realised that Sophy and I might not necessarily have the same father.

'I was thirteen at the time. A bad age for that kind of discovery.'

Lucilla forgot the horror of her nightmare as she listened to him. This was a new side of Nick, a side she knew instinctively he rarely shared with anyone. She ached to reach out and touch him, but she hardly dared breath in case he realised that she was still in his arms and moved away from her. She told herself her behaviour was pitiful and idiotic, but she couldn't help it. Just these few brief moments of physical and mental closeness to him were worth any amount of future suffering.

'What I heard threw me completely; it seemed to answer so many of my own questions, about why my father never seemed to love me the way he did Sophy. I brooded on it . . . ran wild and got myself into all kinds of trouble. I drove my dad's car without a licence and got stopped by the police . . . went around with a wild crowd, most of whom were already into drink and drugs. All of it was really just a bid to get attention, to say to my parents "Look at me, I'm hurting . . ." '

He shook his head. 'They were killed before either of them heard me. I thought it was my fault . . . my behaviour . . . The papers were full of it. Some even said that Dad had deliberately killed them both.

'God knows what would have happened if Gramps hadn't stepped in and taken charge. I loved him, but when he told me he was sending me to England to boarding-school, I thought my love had turned to hate. I fought him every stage of the way, but he stood firm.'

He looked down at Lucilla.

'Gramps taught me to take pride in myself, to be myself, and then, when I'd finally learned that it didn't matter a damn who my father was, that I was a worthwhile person in my own right, he told me that I was a Barrington. Apparently my mother had had blood tests done when I was about five, because she was concerned at my father's rejection of me. He and I both share the same rare blood group, but that knowledge came too late, and I decided that I was going to make a name for myself on my own merits.

'I knew that I couldn't act, that I didn't have any of the Barrington talent worth a row of beans, but by some quirk of fate I shared Gramps's fascination with the wheeling and dealing of finance. I've never ceased being grateful to my grandfather for what he did for me . . . not financially, but in showing me that, Barrington or not, I was a worthwhile human being. It took me a while longer to accept that my father had his own problems and that they weren't my responsibility, to shed the guilt I felt at his and my mother's death.'

Lucilla had long gone past being pleased because he was sharing his past with her.

As his story unfolded, she had gone cold with the realisation of how closely in many ways his past mirrored her own. Nick had seen in her a victim caught in the same trap as himself, and because of that he had reached out to help her. Had he ever really seen her at all, or had she simply been a cause?

With blindingly recalled detail, she remembered what he had said to her when he had first offered her a job.

The nausea inside her grew. What a fool she had been to ever allow herself to dream that she might mean something to him as a person.

'Lucilla, what is it?'

Nick had seen the way her face had changed, and had felt her withdrawal from him, even though she had remained where she was in his arms, the soft weight of her breast pushing tantalisingly against his arm.

He badly wanted to make love to her, to push them both over the edge of their existing relationship and into the heady depths of a more intimate one, but there was too much at stake. He didn't just want her as his lover, but he suspected that the mere thought of making a commitment to him or anyone else would scare her stupid.

'I want you to go.'

The brittleness of her voice did nothing to hide her anger.

It took him by surprise.

'Go?' he repeated.

'Yes. Go. Leave, depart . . .' Lusilla hissed at

him. 'You've done your good deed, Nick . . . made reparation for your guilt, or whatever it is that motivates you. I've seen the light, realised the error of my ways, acknowledged that I'm never going to be a true heir to my mother's talent.'

'Lucilla . . .'

'Don't touch me!'

His hands fell to his sides, and suddenly, dangerously, his anger matched hers, roaring out of control.

'That wasn't what you said in my office this afternoon.'

He regretted the words the moment he spoke them and saw the white sickness invade Lucilla's face. He knew how vulnerable she was, and the last thing he wanted to do was to hurt her, but she had pushed him too far, rejecting all his attempts to get close to her . . . to love her.

'So we shared a kiss. So what?' Lucilla demanded with all the careless insouciance she could muster. As an act, it wasn't very good, her voice wobbled and she couldn't quite meet Nick's eyes.

'It meant nothing,' she lied desperately, adding in a harsh burst of words, 'For God's sake, Nick, you know me better than that. The night we met, I was there to seduce your brother-in-law into giving me a part in his series, and that wasn't the first time, or the first man, by a long chalk. You think you know me, Nick, but you don't, and I'm tired of being on the receiving end of your pity. Let's face it,' she challenged him angrily, 'the only reason I'm here at all is because you

promised Bea you'd look after me. Bea's everyone's ideal woman, isn't she, Nick? But you're
wasting your time there . . . Elliott will never let her
go.'

Several things had struck Nick as he listened to
her, and the one he was clinging to the hardest
was that no woman would try so desperately to
create a false image for a man she cared nothing for
at all.

His expression was hidden from Lucilla, but he
seemed to spend a long time looking down at his
hands, which were linked loosely together.

She missed the warmth of his arms around her,
but she told herself hardily that it was a loss she was
going to have to get used to.

What was it about his linked hands that was
responsible for such frowning concentration?

Nick wasn't even looking at his hands, not really.
What he was doing was trying to judge the extent
of the risk he was about to take. It was incalcul-
able, but he might never have another opportunity
like this one. Already Lucilla was retreating from
him, armouring herself with the brittle indifference
she had exhibited the first time they met.

He took a steadying breath and then said evenly,
'Point one—the reason you're here has nothing
to do with Bea or any promise I made to her, but
is due solely to the fact that I can't bear to let you out
of my sight.

'Point two—your half-sister, charming and lovely
though she is, means nothing to me other than the
fact that she happens to be *your* half-sister, and

I for my sins happen to love you almost to the point
of insanity.

'Point three—that kiss this afternoon which you
so wilfully and wrongly describe as ''nothing''
would have led to us being lovers by now if it
weren't for two very disparate facts. The first is
that I do not intend either now or at any time in
the future to make love to you in my office.'

'In case someone comes in and sees you?' Lucilla
sneered, still not ready to let go of her defences and
trust him.

'No. In case someone come in and sees *you*.'
He saw her face and said softly, 'What do you
think it would do to your credibility as my assistant if
that happened, Lucilla?'

His words hit home, and hard. Colour scorched
her skin. Too often in the past she had been accused
of using sex to promote herself to pretend ignor-
ance.

'What was the other reason?' she asked him
unsteadily.

For a while it seemed as though he wasn't going
to answer her, and over her bunched muscles her
skin started to crawl with tension.

'It involves mutual trust and honesty,' he said
evasively at last. 'And then, looking into rigid
face, he demanded explosively, 'God, Lucilla, do
you really think I'm like all the others? Stupid
enough to be deceived by my own ego and that
come-on pretence you hide behind? If you and
I ever became lovers, it will be because you love
me as I love you, and I promise you it won't be

in my office, where we can be interrupted at any moment. Not for your first time.'

Lucilla looked at him then, and wondered blindly why she had ever doubted him. It was all there in his eye, in his words, in the slightly crooked smile that curled his mouth. But old habits died hard, and she couldn't stop herself from saying tartly, 'Not at any other time either, thank you very much. I want pure cotton sheets, champagne and . . .'

'Oh, God, if you don't stop looking at me like that, I swear to heaven, Lucilla, I'm going to take you in my arms and make love to you right here and now, and to hell with the consequences,' Nick told her, interrupting her ruthlessly.

Her heart was beating so fast that she thought she was going to start hyper-ventilating, but that didn't stop her from fixing her gaze on Nick and keeping it there.

She heard him say harshly, 'Lucilla.'

And then his arms closed round her, and before his mouth touched hers he whispered against her lips, 'I love you, Lucilla.'

She slept far into the morning, only waking when Nick brought in her breakfast and kissed her.

'Still love me?' he asked her whimsically, but she saw the faint shadow of doubt in his eyes and wrapped her arms lovingly around him.

Last night had banished all her fears and doubts, and she had ultimately given herself to him with a whole-hearted commitment that had surprised them both. Now the look he gave her warned her that there was no going back.

'I want you to marry me,' he told her unsteadily after they had exchanged a long kiss.

'Yes,' she told him simply. Already she had travelled a long way, and her belief and trust in him was now so complete that she had no hesitation in showing him her feelings. 'But, Nick, I'm no Bea, nor will I ever be. I want to be your wife, have our children, but I want to work as well. I want to do something for myself. To prove myself, if you like.'

'I agree,' Nick told her firmly. 'I'd like you to stay on and run the agency. I'm a financier, really, and already I've taken too much time off from my real business. Originally I didn't intend to do any more than take over the agency and install someone to run it.'

'But if I run the agency, and you're based in the States . . .'

'I don't have to be,' he asured her quickly. 'I just chose to be because my family are there. I can just as easily base myself in London. In fact, I prefer to. Perhaps because I went to school and university here, I prefer it. Or perhaps it's just that Hollywood still holds sad memories for me. My father's unhappiness seems to linger almost visibly on the air over there.'

'Do you think he deliberately crashed the plane?' Lucilla asked him, not because she was curious about his answer, but because she sensed his need to talk about it.

'I don't honestly know. I know he was capable of doing something like that. At times I've even sensed the same deep vein of dangerous possessiveness in myself. My mother was threatening to divorce him, and yet in many ways he was a very cautious, analytical person. On balance, I think the accident was genuine, but it's something we'll never know.'

'Just as I'll never know whether my mother didn't believe that I was locked in the cupboard, or simply didn't care.'

He leaned over to kiss her again, and the bed-clothes slipped, exposing her breasts. She flushed as she reached to retrieve her protective covering.

Nick laughed and teased her. 'An embarrassed temptress! Don't be ashamed of letting me see you want me, Lucilla,' he told her more soberly. 'Your body isn't.'

And he gently removed the covers and bent to kiss her hard nipples.

The sensation of his mouth against her sensitive flesh reawakened her desire for him. It coiled tautly in her belly and made her reach for him.

Now, at last, she had found surcease from the restless ambitions that had driven her for so long. Now there was no need to struggle to be something she was not. Now, at last, she could simply be herself, and that meant loving Nick and spending her life with him.

Harlequin Presents ®

Coming Next Month

1191   NO WAY TO SAY GOODBYE Kay Gregory
Gareth Mardon closes his Vancouver office and heartlessly dismisses the staff.
Roxane Peters is furious—and she has no compunctions about making her
feelings quite clear to Gareth. Only somehow, it seems, her feelings are
threatened, too....

1192   THE HEAT IS ON Sarah Holland
When Steve Kennedy erupts into Lorel's life, she has the very uncomfortable
feeling she's met him before. Yet it's impossible to ignore him, for he proves to
be the screenwriter on the film in which she wants the leading role.

1193   POTENTIAL DANGER Penny Jordan
Young Kate had been too passionately in love to care about the future. Now a
mature woman, Kate has learned to take care of herself and her daughter. But
no matter how she tries she can't stop loving Silas Edwards, the man who
betrayed her.

1194   DEAL WITH THE DEVIL Sandra Marton
Elena marries Blake Rogan to get out of her revolution-torn country on an
American passport. She believes Rogan married her in a deal with her father
for hard cash. But Rogan just wants to get out alive—with or without Elena.

1195   SWEET CAPTIVITY Kate Proctor
Kidnapped and imprisoned along with famous film director Pascal de
Perregaux, Jackie is prey to all sorts of feelings. Most disturbing is her
desperate attraction to Cal, her fellow victim—especially since he believes she
is in league with their abductors....

1196   CHASE THE DAWN Kate Walker
Desperate for money to restore her little sister's health, Laurel approaches her
identical twin sister's estranged husband. She's forgotten just how much like
her twin she looks—and she finds herself impersonating her sister and
"married" to the formidable Hal Rochester.

1197   DRIVING FORCE Sally Wentworth
Maddy's divorce from racing-car driver West Marriott was painful. He is no
longer part of her life. Now West needs her professional help after an accident.
Maddy isn't sure, though, that she can treat her ex-husband as just
another client!

1198   WHEN THE GODS CHOOSE Patricia Wilson
Arrogant Jaime Carreras is the most insulting man Sara has ever met. Why
should she care what he thinks of her? Unfortunately, however, Jaime is the
only man who can help her trace her father in the wilds of Mexico.

Available in August wherever paperback books are sold, or through
Harlequin Reader Service:

In the U.S.
901 Fuhrmann Blvd.
P.O. Box 1397
Buffalo, N.Y. 14240-1397

In Canada
P.O. Box 603
Fort Erie, Ontario
L2A 5X3

Harlequin Superromance

**Here are the longer, more involving stories you
have been waiting for...Supperromance.**

Modern, believable novels of love, full of the complex
joys and heartaches of real people.

Intriguing conflicts based on today's constantly
changing life-styles.

Four new titles every month.
Available wherever paperbacks are sold.

SUPER-1

Harlequin Regency Romance™

Romance the way it was *always* meant to be!

The time is 1811, when a Regent Prince rules the empire. The place is London, the glittering capital where rakish dukes and dazzling debutantes scheme and flirt in a dangerously exciting game. Where marriage is the passport to wealth and power, yet every girl hopes secretly for love....

Welcome to Harlequin Regency Romance where reading is an adventure and romance is *not* just a thing of the past! Two delightful books a month.

Available wherever Harlequin Books are sold.

REG-1R

LOST

MOON FLOWER

TO BE FOUND . . .
lots of romance & adventure
in Harlequin's
3000th Romance

THE LOST MOON FLOWER
Bethany Campbell

Available wherever Harlequin Books
are sold this August.

MOON-1B

"NEW"

Harlequin Historicals

Storytelling at its best
by some of your favorite authors such as
Kristen James, Nora Roberts, Cassie Edwards

Strong, independent heroines
Heroes you'll fall in love with
Compelling love stories

History has never been so romantic.

Look for them now wherever Harlequin Books are sold.

HIST-L-1RR